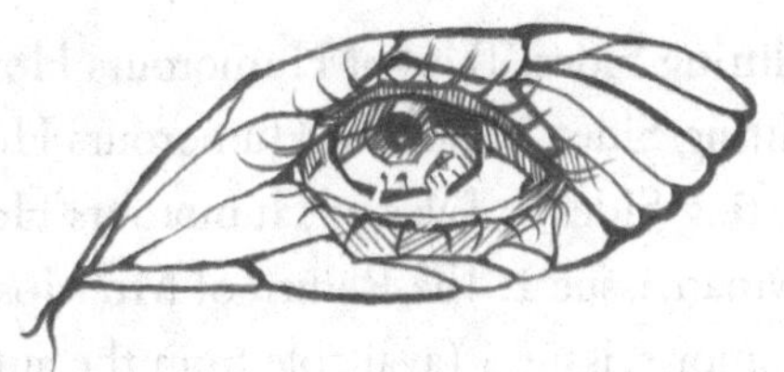

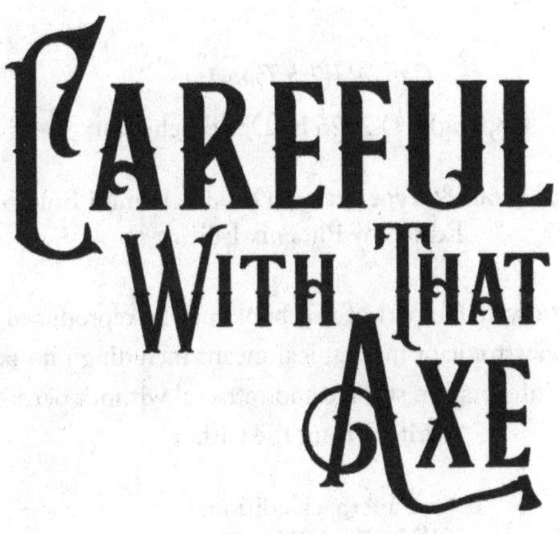

CAREFUL WITH THAT AXE

DAVID SCHEMBRI

North Forest
BOOKS

My Claire first published in Issue 15 of Midnight Echo by the Australiasian Horror Writers Association, 2020. Edited by Lee Murray.

Sister of Charity published in Trickster's Treats 3 by Things in the Well, 2019. Edited by Marie O'Regan and Lee Murray.

Shadow and Fire first published in Issue 14 of Spectral Realms by Hippocampus Press – New York, 2021. Edited by S.T. Joshi. 2022 Recommendations for Best Horror #14-long list by Ellen Datlow.

Destiny first published in Issue 17 of Spectral Realms by Hippocampus Press – New York, 2022. Edited by S.T. Joshi.

Ghost first published by Silver Blade Magazine, 2022. Edited by John C. Mannone.

Soul in Chains first published in Issue 13 of Midnight Echo by the Australiasian Horror Writers Association, 2018. Edited by Paul Mannering.

The Land of the Stolen Children first published in Issue 23 of Spectral Realms by Hippocampus Press – New York, 2025. Edited by S.T. Joshi.

The Great Invocation first published in the Black Beacon Book of Horror by Black Beacon Books, 2023. Edited by Cameron Trost.

For my siblings, Carmen, Rosy, Ray and Jim.
You have all inspired me in your own special way.

Contents

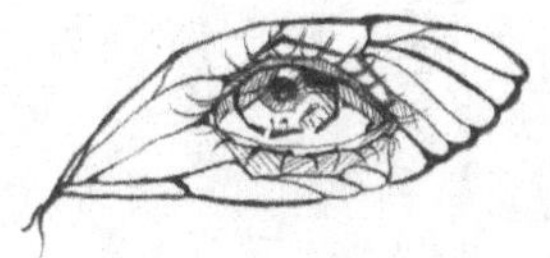

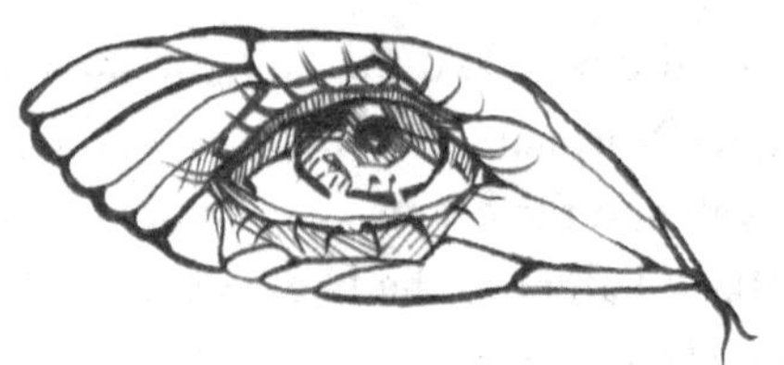

INTRODUCTION

Come with me, dear sir, simply follow my voice…

Now, imagine if you will, a place where worlds collide with imagination, and the two create something both strange and disturbing. You have arrived.

David Schembri, Dave to his many friends, is a writer who takes you into his darkness, and trust us, you'd never guess just how dark things can get. From the worst of humanity to a fear you didn't expect, this collection encompasses everything you could possibly imagine. Even better, with an added 20,000 words there's now even more to bite into. We found ourselves captivated, unable to stop reading at night and get some sleep.

Even amongst a collection as great as this, there are a few stand-out stories. These are a few that stay in my memory to this day.

'The Unforgiving Court' begins the book with a look at just how evil men can be brought to account, even if it takes some supernatural help.

'The Reconstruction of Melissa' tears you a new one, the sound of flesh parting from sinew and bone redolent throughout the piece. Be prepared.

'The Fifty Mile House' takes my favourite genre, military horror, and makes it something both beautiful and disturbing, dragging you in further than you thought possible.

And these are, as I said, just a few. Really, there's not an average story in here. They are all good.

Of special note is the Dark Tales of Christmas section, where bad Santa permeates the holiday cheer. That festive season will never be the same again. You have been warned.

Dave is one of the best writers in Australian horror, as well as being a damn fine artist and designer. He's been a part of the Australian horror scene for a long time now, and his experience shows in his writing. He has a way of dragging you into his stories, and believe me, once you get there you just want to escape alive.

As a bonus, Dave's original art gives you another view into the author's imagination. Nothing beats seeing just what the writer imagined when he wrote 'that' scene. You'll know what I mean when you get to it. The art is of a simplistic style, but the subject of each piece touches a visceral part of the human psyche, causing a frisson to run through you when viewed as part of the story its inspired by. The art ads an entire new dimension to the experience.

Apart from the exceptional prose, the poetry is another added pleasure. Not normally readers of poetry, we both found these hit hard, the language accessible yet poignant.

All up, Dave has written (and drawn) a winner here, and we think it will take a lot of people by surprise when it's released. This is a great collection that deserves to be read.

Geoff Brown & Dawn Roach – Cohesion Press

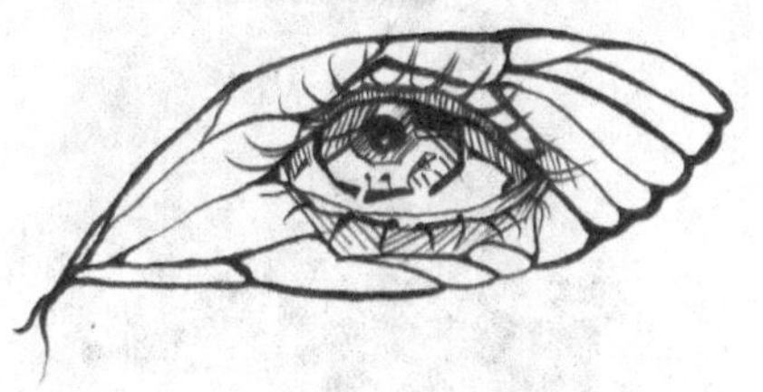

The Unforgiving Court

There is a fear of things that dash from tree to tree,
In haunted places where creatures bear no breath.
To be caught seeing their skin, scarred and pale,
Is an Omen for certain Death.

Umschlagplatz, Warsaw Ghetto, 1941.

The boxcars loomed in the distance before a sea of petrified faces. Fabiane's hand was hot in Edmund's grip as they were forced along the flow of the crowd. Helina, their daughter, cried in-between them, clasping her suitcase to her chest. The whistle of the black steam locomotive pierced the air. German infantry and SS officers had begun to penetrate the masses. Edmund looked on in horror as everyone was divided. Machine-gun fire cracked as warning shots were blasted into the sky. "Stay close!" Edmund yelled to his family.

The condemned were being sent to the left and right of the platform. Edmund saw the boxcars, normally used to transport cattle, being filled with terrified civilians.

"What is happening?" Fabiane cried.

Edmund looked deep into her eyes. He had never seen her so pale, so frightened. "Help us, Papa?" Helina begged and he drew her close and kissed her hard on the forehead.

The division had reached them.

"No!" Fabiane screamed when her shoulder was grabbed.

Edmund held his grip firm and Fabiane surged towards him. A soldier's gloved fist met her jaw. Edmund looked on in terror as the trooper shoved her away. He cried with Helina as they watched Fabiane scream back at them, her arm raised to the sky as if she were drowning. "*Edmund! Edmund! Helina!*"

"I love you!" Edmund cried, but before he knew it, Helina was snatched from him also, shoved into the flow that claimed his wife.

Edmund was forced to follow a surge of countrymen to the right.

He could still hear their screams when he was loaded onto a truck.

The treacherous journey went on for what seemed like days. It was enough to shake one's bones to the point of breaking. Two German troopers, clad in winter coats and with rifles strapped over their shoulders, rode against the tailgate. They stood against the backdrop of a red dawn that felt like the entrance to hell itself.

The crank and squeal of the brakes shook everyone. Startled from a somnolent daze, Edmund looked upon the bemused faces of his countrymen. The two troopers leapt off the tailgate and their boots hit snow. Edmund looked upon the snow as it fell from the heavens.

The heavens that had forsaken them all.

He could hear German voices in the surrounds. A gate was opened. The truck's engines were throttled again, and barbed-wire fences passed by. Through the haze of falling snow, Edmund could see troops closing the gates. The truck stopped, and the engine was killed. His head ached at the sudden absence of the roaring motor that had thundered his ears for so many long hours. The tailgate was dropped, and they were ordered out.

Edmund was seated close to the rear, so he was one of the first to exit. They were all lined up, hands on heads, along the length of the beast that had taken them so far. Four soldiers stood before them. Edmund looked beyond their helmets to see a decent occupation of German military. Mostly infantry soldiers, either marching along the boundaries or towards what looked to be a large, two-storey building. The haze of snowfall clouded the hefty Swastika flags that waved lazily from the rooftops, and the flag of Nazi Germany centred between them – high and proud atop a small bell tower.

Edmund was scared to his very marrow. He wondered what Fabiane and Helina would be seeing. One of the soldiers marched toward them, selected two from the line-up and led them out of sight. Soon, two more troopers appeared escorting an SS officer – tall, thin, and wearing distaste upon his face. His coat was double-breasted and secured with gold buttons and a thick, black leather belt. A Luger automatic pistol was holstered at his hip, along with accompanying pouches, housing ammunition no doubt.

He walked slowly to Edmund's end of the line with his hands casually crossed behind his back. He walked down the line-up with eyes of piercing inspection.

"I am SS Commandant Gotifried Harrer. This is my Weimar Headquarters. To the south of this site is the labour camp of Buchenwald. Here, we need a labourer. You have been brought to me because you are all farmers!" he said and reclaimed his position.

The two countrymen returned, rolling a large, freshly-sawn slab of a pine tree. An axe was dropped onto the wood and the men hurried back into line.

"Take the axe. Have two attempts. Once you have taken your turn, step back into line at once! I will decide who will work to survive," said Harrer.

In that moment, a soldier grabbed the man next to Edmund – the first in line – and thrust him before the slab. The man grabbed the axe in trembling hands. Edmund looked on as two quick cuts were made. The countryman dropped the axe and ran back into line.

It was Edmund's turn.

Shoved towards the slab, he held the axe as firmly as he could. In all of his fear, he looked at the slab as it was being lightly covered in snowfall. He eyed the knots in the grain. Edmund had chopped many slabs of wood in his time and knew where to aim. He feared that two attempts would not be enough.

"*Hacken!*" ordered Harrer.

Edmund quivered and raised the axe and put as much might into his first attack as he could. He aimed away from the knots, and created a deep fissure in the left quarter of the pine. He steadied his footing, and with the faces of his family embedded in his mind, swung again. Splinters flew as the left portion of the slab was cut clear. He kept his eyes shut and exhaled, almost crying, and let the axe fall from his grasp. To survive would leave hope, no matter how small, to see his family again.

Before Edmund reclaimed his place, Harrer shouted, "Halt!"

Edmund frozen.

"*Gesicht mir!*"

Edmund obeyed and turned, his trembling hands instinctively raised above his shoulders.

Harrer gestured a harsh finger, ordering for Edmund to stand aside. Edmund did so and was held clear of the soldiers before the line-up. Then the echoing voice of the Nazi shouted, "*Feuer auf mein Kommando!*"

Edmund whimpered; he had learnt how to speak German from his father. Having traded with German farmers it was customary to learn the language. He knew what Harrer had just ordered. The soldier behind him shoved his shoulder as if to silence him, yet Edmund continued to whimper.

"*Feuer!*"

The crack of rifle fire erupted, reducing the countrymen into a line of motionless bodies in the snow.

Edmund's vision blurred through his tears. Harrer stepped before him. "Your duties here will be to collect and chop wood to feed the fireplaces within the Headquarters. Store your wood by the rear door in the provided bucket for the house attendants to retrieve. If you are seen doing anything other than your duties, if the attendants complain of not having sufficient wood, you will be executed. Food and water will be supplied once a day. Your quarters are located to the west behind you."

Edmund nodded before being left alone, cold and petrified.

It took several moments before he had the courage to roll the pine west. As he laboured with the wood, he burdened himself with the axe beneath his arm. Edmund eyed the building to his right. Its geometric architecture looked newly-built with perfect ninety-degree angles. White boards, and a tall tiled roofline with four chimneys reaching for the angry sky. The further he pushed on, the more he thought of Fabiane and Helina. It had been over two days since he last saw them.

He reached the rear of the house and stood gasping. A shelter, little more than a shack fit to house firewood, stood before him. He slid open the door, stumbled in and looked at the interior. There were holes in the roof and the walls were made of rusted sheeting. His heart sank further when he saw a makeshift bed to his left, crudely constructed from timber. Upon it was some damp bedding – a single army blanket and a small pillow. He noticed some writing on the outer panelling of the door painted white in large letters:

Arbeit Macht Frei.

Work brings freedom.

The floor of the shelter was the ground itself, muddy with melted snow. The wind whistled through the many holes in the walls, and he wrapped his arms around himself and shivered. Before long, he decided to inspect the exterior. A small port, with a single piece of sheeting for a roofline, housed an old wood cart and a small assortment of rusted saws.

He then braved the wood bucket by the rear of the Headquarters. He trudged his way over and noticed to his left that soldiers were walking in and out of a single-storey building. Their barracks, he guessed.

To his surprise, the bucket was full by the rear door. He couldn't help but think that someone else had died to fill it. He then noticed the nearby woodlands further south. He knew with heartache that Fabiane and Helina were imprisoned within the distance.

He spent hours thinking of the sign that was painted crudely on the boxcars that had swallowed them.

Buchenwald, it read.

Edmund kept working until night and cold demanded he stop. He was exhausted when he entered the darkness of his shelter. He dropped to the bed that may as well have been made out of a slab of stone. He listened to the thud of his broken heart, the ache of his bones, and the painful rumble in his stomach.

The sounds of commotion shook Edmund from his troubled sleep. Light glared in through the many holes in his shelter and he rose. Many voices shouted from the barracks. The young soldiers were yelling words like, "*Dämons!*" and, "*Abschaum!*"

He rubbed his eyes. He didn't know how long he had lain down before sleep had finally taken him. He struggled to his feet and cautiously looked out the door to see soldiers rallying.

Something was disturbingly wrong.

He hauled himself out the door. With his strength waning, he wheeled the wood cart towards the barracks, darting glances back and forth from the Headquarters to the commotion. He paused when he noticed two soldiers drag something from the barracks – a body? He quickly went to the bucket when he saw Harrer appear with his escorts. Edmund hurriedly busied himself with the wood.

He didn't dare turn his head for fear of being caught

spying, but he listened.

"In den Wald sofort!" Harrer ordered after seeing what the soldiers had dragged out.

Immediately, at least two dozen soldiers followed their Commandant's orders and charged into the nearby woodlands. Edmund's heart was pounding. He listened to the Commandant grunting distasteful theories to other SS officers who greeted him before he entered the Headquarters. Notions of '*Polish Resistance*' gritted through his teeth, and '*Worthless guerrilla operations, we will find and burn them all!*'

Within moments, the courtyard behind the Headquarters was deserted. Edmund feared to venture forth, but he couldn't help but investigate what had spooked the great army. He wheeled his wood cart over to the crude figure in the snow and gasped. What he thought was a charred corpse was nothing of the sort, and it left him filled with dread and confusion.

The object in the snow was a life-sized wooden carving of a man. There was no face, just the grain, but the mimicking of limbs and head were in accurate proportion. The etching into the wood looked to have been crafted with fine, sharp tools. The grooves worked in all directions across and through the grain, suggesting to him that the carving had been done in extreme haste. He did not know what to make of it.

He wheeled his cart back to the shelter when he heard distant gunfire from the forest.

Edmund spent the next hour chopping the pine slabs that were scattered behind his shelter. He was running low and had no idea how he was going to obtain more. He was too petrified to enter the woods for fear of being shot. His entire duty seemed hopeless to him. When he turned, there was Harrer and his men, watching him.

He dropped his axe and stood to attention.

"*Essen! Wasser!*" Harrer spat.

Food and water had been brought.

"Your supply is obtained in the Ettersberg Hills behind you! You will have a guard with you at all times. Attempt to escape and you will be shot!"

A third soldier then marched from behind the trio and stood to attention before the Commandant.

"The prisoner is to bring in three carts of wood before nightfall. If he fails, you are to shoot him in the courtyard before the barracks!"

"*Ja, Kommandant!*" the soldier yelled.

Harrer and his escorts departed, leaving Edmund alone with his possible executioner.

The journey into the Ettersberg Hills was slow. It was almost impossible for him to push the old cart through the dense scrub. He looked towards the tangled woods ahead and sighted a fallen tree. He rested for a moment, eyeing the soldier and the rifle the man held in gloved hands: the same weapon he had seen in the hands of most German soldiers.

"*Umzug auf!*"

The soldier stabbed north with his weapon.

Edmund's tree was up a small rise to the west. He had to say something, so he spoke in German to the young man, the boy.

"I must leave the cart here and roll wood down to it. I will take my saw up with me."

The soldier's face grew pale.

"Nein! North!"

Edmund threw his hands in the air.

"North!"

He quickly moved his cart north and continued the laborious journey. He couldn't set eyes on a boy so polluted by obvious hatred.

When Edmund found more fallen trees, he rested his cart and went to work.

For hours he cut and chopped and cut and chopped. The surrounds of the forest were disturbingly still compared to the strong winds he would suffer when returning a cartload to the shelter. The small portions of bread and water were hardly enough to keep up his strength, but he pressed on.

As he cut into a second tree, he caught the soldier looking at him eagerly, as if interested in his labours. The soldier would behave dismissively in those instances. Edmund sensed humanity in the boy and kept an eye on him.

When he had emptied a second load and ventured back, the commotion of the returning infantry stopped him in his tracks. The soldiers were rallying into the courtyard. Their captain stopped and noticed Edmund's guard and yelled. "The barracks! Fifteen minutes!"

Edmund's face went pale and chills covered him.

He knew he would never fill the cart in that time. It was over. Having any chance of surviving to see Fabiane and Helina again were gone. He had failed, and he suddenly fell to his knees and broke into tears.

The soldier stood over him and ordered him to stand. When he didn't move, the boy gripped his shoulder and lifted him to his feet. Edmund was shoved towards the woodlands and could feel the butt of the soldier's rifle pressed against his back. Edmund thought that he was to be shot in the courtyard, but what did it matter… Back at the work site Edmund turned to face his executioner, who had shouldered his weapon. "You can still fill your cart," he began. "I can help you. *Schnell*, it will be dark soon!"

The boy didn't wait for him to utter a word. He positioned himself on the other end of the saw that was wedged in a trunk and waited for him to take his position.

"Schnell!"

Edmund was shocked at the sudden benevolence of the boy. He soon took his place and they worked together.

By twilight the cart was back at the shelter for inspection like nothing had happened.

The following morning; the same commotion.

Edmund didn't venture out into the courtyard, but witnessed the same events take place. Another carved figure was dragged out of the barracks accompanied by the panicked voices of the armed Hitler youth. Yet again, Harrer ordered his infantry to raid the forest in search of the guerrillas. The Nazi seemed more furious and his voice was full of the aggression of a madman.

Edmund noticed a soldier was marching his way, and he knew that it was his guard, his saviour… When the soldier stood to attention before him, he said, "The same drill as yesterday. *Schnell!*"

They ventured back into the Ettersberg Hills. At the work site they heard the distant crack of gunfire. Edmund felt compelled to say something.

"Is the compound being raided by a resistance?" he asked as he steadied himself before the saw.

The soldier took a few moments, looked about himself as if to make sure there were no onlookers and immediately shouldered his weapon.

"There is *no* resistance," he whispered.

"*Nein?* Then an army, *ja?* Invaders?"

"Invaders. *Ja.*"

He drew back his saw and began to cut. He stopped and looked at the boy watching him.

"My name is Edmund. What's yours?"

The soldier looked about himself again.

"Julius," he whispered.

"Your orders were to kill me, Julius. Why didn't you?"

Julius shrugged, but Edmund knew the answer. Julius was just as ensnared as a soldier as Edmund was a prisoner.

"Thank you, Julius. It was very kind of you."

Julius looked at him and displayed the hint of a grin. "I can help, *Ja?*"

Edmund nodded.

Julius stepped down to the other end of the saw keenly and they went to work. They cut pine together into the dying morning. They rolled the slabs to a more level part of the forest floor for Edmund to chop. Of course, Julius showed interest in having a turn with the axe. "Have you ever used an axe before?" Edmund asked him.

"*Nein.* I grew up in Berlin. I have never been on a farm."

"Be careful."

Suddenly, they paused to a disturbing sound in the west – a scream? They could hear sounds of someone whimpering between bursts of agony. Edmund and Julius looked at each other and went down the pathway they had grooved through the forest. Edmund stared up the hill, to the very first tree he had wanted to cut. The screams were heard again. They were close, just on the other side.

Edmund motioned to venture up.

"*Nein!* Don't go up there!"

"Someone sounds hurt, Julius. We must try and see if they need our help."

"*Nein!* We can't go *near* there. It's a haunted place!" Julius whispered harshly.

"I don't understand. How do you mean haunted? The person suffering could be one of your friends. What has been happening at the barracks, Julius? You seem to know something that no one else does."

"It has been happening for weeks. Soldiers are being kidnapped. Taken from their bunks. Left in their place, beneath their blankets, is a wooden carving to mimic them. The Commandant believes it's the work of a Polish guerrilla operation. So do the men, but not me."

"What do *you* think is happening to—"

Suddenly, the scream again, and Edmund walked up the hill.

"We must keep out of sight!" Julius whispered from behind.

They reached the fallen moss-covered log and kept themselves hidden. Heard from beyond were different noises accompanying the torment. The sounds suggested that swooping ravens were cutting the air. Edmund and Julius stared at each other and shared their trepidation. Edmund decided to peer over the log to get a view of the activity. At first, he saw nothing but forest. Then he noticed a road dwindling off in the distance, which appeared to be nothing more than a track. The forest was clearer down that way, leading into a field of earth mounds.

Edmund was protected from sight by the cover of long grasses from the other side, that in turn, obstructed his view of the swooping and suffering. He leaned in carefully and separated the grasses with his hands and looked upon a sight that nearly made him collapse.

It *was* a German soldier. He had been stripped of his clothing from the waist up. Tied to a tree, his hands were bound over his head. His torso was covered in bloodied, deep lacerations, and his legs shook and twitched to his obvious misery. Edmund then saw the bird-like creatures swooping from the treetops, and every time, they left the soldier with another cut to his chest and belly.

"Don't let them see you!" Julius urged, tugging at Edmund's coat.

"They are only birds."

"*Nein!*"

Edmund looked closer and his head swam.

They were not birds. Some settled on the soldier's chest, with their talons dug into his flesh.

The creatures looked to be humanoids of small stature. They were pale-skinned, naked, and had diaphanous wings – veined and crude in nature. More of them were suspended on the soldier's body, hanging from his skin and beginning to rip at it, boring into him. The screams of the soldier intensified as the malicious… *daemons?*… all flocked and covered him. The voices coming from their fang-filled little mouths resembled the sounds of enjoyment, as if their actions were designed for entertainment.

The creatures perched on the soldier's head plucked out his eyes. The screams were cut short. Edmund dry retched as he witnessed the humanoids rip open the soldier's belly and begin to mercilessly and playfully pull out his intestines and stomach. The others that were swarmed on his head soon had it dislodged from the neck and were bathing in the fountain of blood from whence it sat. The humanoids continued to strip the corpse, revealing rib bones and spine, their little mouths feasting merrily. Their faces held an angelic beauty that was hauntingly seductive, even as blood covered them. Delicate little tongues licked. Glowing eyes gleamed beneath perfect brows.

"Not birds," Julius whispered.

"Nein. Not birds… but what?"

Edmund felt winded due to the horror he had witnessed. Scarcely able to stand, Julius held his arm as they walked back to the work site. He slumped to the ground, resting his back onto the trunk of a tree. Julius offered him his canteen. "Finish it. I can get more later."

He drank slowly and already felt better as the cool liquid flowed down his dry throat. Julius searched one of the larger pouches on his belt and produced some bread. "Here, eat."

"I-I don't want to get you into trouble, Julius."

"Who will know? Eat. You need it."

After Edmund had eaten the small portion of bread, more than his normal ration, he felt his strength returning.

"What are those creatures?"

Julius sat next to him and brought out a small leather-bound book that was tucked beneath his trousers. He opened it and flipped through several handwritten pages.

"Yours?" Edmund asked.

"My father's. This is his journal. My father is a poet and a professor of Celtic folklore. I share the same passion."

"You want to be a poet?"

"*Ja*. I wish I could be studying now, but the war started. My father gave me his journal to read, so I can remember that the world is full of different things… magical things."

"Magic?"

"Listen…

"In a dark time within heaven's skies,

"In burned the angels' rebellion to threaten God's power,
"Banished from the white gates, now said to be locked,
"In their corpses' graves 'tis said they cower..."

"What does that mean?"

"Do you believe in faeries, Edmund?"

Edmund huffed. "Just imagination. Old stories of make-believe."

"Do you really believe that after what you saw?"

"Tell me what I saw?"

"They used to be alive, Edmund. Like you and me. They were people that had met a horrible death. In the west, did you see a clearing in the forest?"

"*Ja.*"

"Burial mounds, Edmund. Mass graves. The people buried there died not long ago and God has closed the gates on them. Heaven is only for pure and peaceful spirits."

"How can our Maker deny our passage home?"

Julius flipped through the book again. "My father wrote here, and he quotes from an old English scroll, that centuries ago the angels rebelled against him. God banished them and any others he suspected. The ones who are buried in those mounds are full of more than just sorrow, but also anger and grief. They are bound to it, and God knows this and has locked them out. So, denied passage and not being evil spirits, they were also denied entry into hell. Caught in-between, these spirits descended back to Earth and are bound to their burial site. Reincarnated from denoted angels into the creatures you saw feasting."

"Faeries?"

"*Ja*, but of a different kind… There are many sorts, but these are written about here in my father's journal. They are not spirits and they are not alive, but they are physical."

"Julius, none of this makes any sense. They were angels, and now they have been reincarnated, but they are not alive? What are they?"

"Edmund, they are the undead breed of the Unforgiving Court."

Edmund rose from his place and looked west to where he saw the creatures. Another horrific thought suddenly struck his mind, ringing his ears.

"When you told me that bodies are buried in those mounds, then where have they come from?"

Julius directed his eyes out towards the northern sky, to the smoke that rose from Buchenwald. Edmund looked there too.

"They are bodies that couldn't be burned in the crematorium of the concentration camp."

"Crematorium? Harrer said it was a *labour* camp!"

Julius shook his head mournfully. "*Nein, Edmund.* I was stationed there for a year before coming here. People die in Buchenwald every day. Many are executed or worked to death in the quarry. Bodies are piled and burned, and when the corpses are too many, they are loaded onto trucks, and buried in the mounds."

"My wife and daughter are in that camp!"

"I am so sorry, Edmund. I wish I could do something. If only I could…"

Edmund cried into his hands. Julius went to him and placed a hand on his shoulder. "You should not give up hope.

They may yet still be alive. You must hold onto that."

Edmund wished he could believe it, but for the warning in his heart that told him hope was lost.

Julius put his book away. "Edmund?"

He looked up with a swelling face of devastation.

"We are losing daylight. *Schnell...*"

Edmund wiped his face and got up. "Julius, if you were ordered to kill me, would you?"

Julius shrugged.

They worked and met the quota.

A soldier named Anton was the next to be taken. The day after that was Rommel. Then came Albert, Fritz, Karl and Hermann. The piles of wooden stand-ins were burned after the number had reached a dozen. Julius said that the custom behind the crude carvings were the indicators of the faeries' prankish nature.

"To toy with the living is a common source of enjoyment, but with the Unforgiving Court, they have far more deadly behaviours."

Edmund and Julius continued their labours every day for the next three weeks. They talked about the details of the journal, and Edmund came to understand more about the undead, the winged creatures that had chosen the barracks as their playground.

"Make no mistake, the Unforgiving Court have no sides. They would kill anything, anyone," Julius said during a break.

"So they are not vengeful? You would think they would be."

"The spirit that went to heaven was not the same one that was stuck in-between worlds. *Nein, Edmund.* They are the remainders of the spirit. The bad part. They are left bound to their mounds, to the Otherworld they have burrowed beneath the earth."

"They live underground?"

"It is their territory. They would harm anyone who goes near them. Anyone who sees them, anyone who touches the earth they deem sacred."

"What do you think will happen? Will they just keep taking one soldier at a time, or start doing worse?"

"My father quoted from old Scottish folklore that this court is familiar to the *Unseelie Court* faeries. They have a shared liking in bringing harm to humans for entertainment, and that they are *trooping* creatures."

"Like an army?"

"*Ja, Edmund, ja!* These creatures are just playing, soon they will—"

"They are going to attack the compound?"

"That would fit their customs. It may happen soon."

"They will kill all of us."

Julius stood and stared down at Edmund. "Not if you have the deterrents."

"You can repel them?"

"Just wear any item of clothing inside out."

"Sounds ridiculous."

"Any faerie creature, be it spirit, angel or undead, would regard this as being detrimental. I wear all of my undergarments backwards. They work just like a protective charm!"

Julius retrieved a slice of bread from one of his pouches and gave it to him.

"Thank you," said Edmund.

"No! Don't eat it!"

"Why not? I am starving."

"Keep *that* piece of bread in your pocket. The prototype of food, a symbol of life, is also another protection against them!"

"Is this why you have not been kidnapped?"

"I would like to think so."

Edmund tucked the bread into his coat pocket.

"There is another thing all faerie creatures have in common. They are all bound by one weakness."

"I cannot imagine what."

"To utter a faerie's name could summon it to you and you could force it to do your bidding."

"Even these flesh eaters?"

"*Ja, Edmund.* But, of course, one would need to get close enough to hear them speak and live to tell the tale, but I don't think anyone has…"

Edmund remembered the feasting creatures and their little voices. He couldn't recall any words that meant anything to him. Edmund and Julius resumed with another hard day of labour.

Screams echoed in the distance.

Edmund stopped dead in his tracks.

Harrer and his escorts were waiting. Julius stood to

attention before them. Harrer stepped before Julius and looked him up and down with a grimace. "Do you take me for a fool?"

"*Nein, Kommandant!*"

Harrer immediately stepped before Edmund and threw a hard, closed fist into his jaw. Harrer, all the while, had his eyes locked on Julius' face and could see the boy jolt.

"We are at war! Yet you mingle with the enemy? Do you believe in your country and your *Führer!*"

"*Ja, Kommandant!*"

Harrer stepped back and ordered Edmund to face the forest on his knees with his hands behind his head.

Edmund trembled into position.

"Do you realize that we are under attack! Rebels are taking your fellow countrymen and skinning them alive! *Savages!* And I receive intelligence that you are mingling with this prisoner! I have no time for the weak-minded. Do you hear me?"

"*Ja, Kommandant!*"

Through the movements in the snow, Edmund could sense that Julius was forced to remove his helmet and stand behind him, a few steps away.

"*Feuer auf mein Kommando!*"

A trail of urine streamed down Edmund's leg and he cried as Julius' breaths became rapid. A gun, perhaps a pistol, was heard being drawn from its holster.

"*Feuer…*" Harrer's voice was heard, but only in a whisper.

"Please, Kommandant," Julius whimpered. "I can't…"

"*Feuer!*"

"I just want to go home to my father… to my—"

A single gunshot pierced the air.

A splash of something warm draped the back of Edmund's neck. He then felt the weight of a body drop over him. Edmund cried to see Julius' beautiful face stare lifelessly up at the twilight sky.

Harrer shoved Edmund down to the snow and landed a hard boot into his belly. "Bury this mess in the mounds," he ordered as he holstered his pistol.

Edmund stared at the blood flowing out of Julius' head.

His young friend's body was stripped of his weapon belt, helmet, coat and boots. Edmund was then left alone with the corpse as if it were a molested doll. The journal was gone; it would no doubt find a home in one of the fireplaces. A life-long account of histories about the unknown would be for no eyes to see. He knelt beside Julius; it was the first time Edmund had seen his hair – Julius had never removed his helmet. Fine, golden strands swayed lazily in the cold breeze.

Edmund cried and stroked them before loading his friend into the cart.

Edmund chose to bury Julius at the work site. The place where they became friends. He didn't dare go to the mounds as he knew he would not return. He buried Julius beneath the pine they were cutting together. He even carved a small memorial into the wood.

Julius the Poet, 1941.

When night came, Edmund laid down on the makeshift bed within his shelter for hours. He tried to focus through his sorrow. He tried to remember. He thought about the little snarling creatures feeding on the soldier's corpse. He tried to remember what was spitting from their tiny, bloodied tongues.

Edmund mouthed and mouthed for hours. He was whispering the same grouping of letters over and over again.

Faf-nir. Faff-nirrr… Fafnir…

Was it right, he wondered?

Was he uttering a faerie's name?

Edmund was startled in the darkness, only pierced by a few beams of moonlight. He heard a scratch at the iron and he jolted again. He fell back into his bed and pulled the blanket up to his chest.

The scratching continued all around him, as if something were circling the iron structure with the tip of a bayonet. Edmund trembled as his eyes followed the rapid assault on his walls. It stopped suddenly.

Through a hole near the roofline above his feet, he saw two sets of tiny claws. He held his breath at the emergence of a small head. It glowed with the aid of the moonlight.

The tiny face of womanly beauty tilted sideways as its eyes caught sight of him. A small squeak, with likeness to a rat, came from the creature before it pushed itself noisily through the hole and hovered down to his legs. When it landed, its crude wings fluttered to a stop and folded behind its hunched back.

Edmund feared these Unforgiving Court creatures of the damned, but having one creep over his stomach was another horror altogether. Its pale skin glowed in the dark and was mapped with scars. Yet the matted flesh weaved into a smooth, almost delicate, draping of skin over its shoulders and neck. The face did look female, yet no other features on the creature could determine sex. No breasts or any detail between its legs. Edmund was shocked he had the courage to allow his eyes to wander. Its thin line of blue lips was parted slightly to reveal a hint of tangled jaws, gleaming. The hair on its head was dreaded with dirt and clotted blood. It approached in a quick succession of steps until it was at Edmund's nose. He tried not to yelp as the creature hissed, *Fafffff-nnnnnniiiirrrrr!*

Edmund shook where he lay with the faerie panting. It soon let out a small growl of impatience, its beauty transforming, and thrashed a claw at his right cheek, drawing blood. Edmund jolted, and Fafnir squealed and flew up out of reach. As Edmund stood, he looked about fearfully, shielding his face the whole time with his forearm. After a moment, Fafnir hovered down slowly from the darkness and settled before him.

Fafff! Nnnnirr!

Edmund lowered his arm from his face. Fafnir's gaze was

hypnotic, replaced again by the slender façade. The creature was doing something to him. He felt a heat in his chest and throat, then in his skull. A sensation like nothing felt before was moving through his body like a warm haze. It settled his nerves and sorrow. All he could think of then was what his heart truly desired.

Fafnir…

Edmund gulped. "I-I command you to sa-save my wife and daughter."

Fafnir's face grimaced, growled and hissed as if in protest, its face of horror returning, as if it was turned inside out. Edmund felt the warmth of the faerie's magic leave him and then the weight of his sorrow returned. He felt that Fafnir's response could only mean that the task was not possible. Fafnir circled, hissed and flew out a larger hole in the shelter.

He listened to the creature's departing flight as it entered the darkness of the Ettersberg Hills.

Dawn.

Edmund went back to the work site and did nothing. He simply sat at Julius' grave. He picked at the snow. He cried for his family. He listened to the branches above creak eerily. He listened to the distant gunfire as soldiers searched for the guerrillas.

When the day finally died he walked back to the shelter with his empty cart. He expected to find Harrer and his escorts. But there was no one.

He could not help but wonder.

Edmund jolted at a knock at the iron door. He could see the beams of a flashlight pierce the darkness from the outside.

He rose, guessing that his execution had been saved for the night. He took a breath and slid open the door. The man before him was an SS officer, but no one he had seen before. Whoever it was, he said nothing. He simply stood in the doorway with a torch in one hand and something else in the other. Edmund thought it was a pistol, but then the officer brought it up to his mouth and drank from it. He swayed slightly as he wiped his mouth. "Where is your hospitality? Stand aside."

"This shelter is not fit for your grace."

The officer huffed and stepped in. Edmund slid the door closed as the officer dumped the torch on the ground. They stood within a meter of each other. The officer's breath smelt of whisky. He slumped down on the hard bed and grunted in disgust. Edmund stood silent. The officer took another sip from his silver flask and burped. "Your name?"

"Edmund."

"Your *full* name!"

Edmund's heart raced.

"E-Edmund Mieszro Adamski."

The officer seemed to relax again and took in another drink.

"*I*, am Commandant Von Ludendorff."

"Heil Hitler…" Edmund said. He didn't know what else to say and his gut churned when he said it. He extended his right arm straight in front of himself to mimic the Nazi salute.

Ludendorff stared.

He then burst out into laughter. Edmund's arm lowered slowly as he watched the Commandant snort and chortle. This display made Edmund fear every passing second. He felt belittled and was expecting to die at any second.

"Do you know why I am drinking?"

"*Nein, Kommandant.*"

"To honour my family. I have four children. A wife too. They are in Heidelberg… safe. I had leave planned for a month to see them… it has just been denied by the Chancellor. I am to continue my duties for the war effort. It has been two years since I last saw my family. My youngest son has just turned five years old… My government can't even give me one month… so, forgive me if I do not return the greeting."

Ludendorff took another drink. "I take it that you have your own tragedies to bear?"

"*Ja.*"

"Mine would seem small in comparison, I know. But I didn't come here to offload my burdens, I have come for your help."

"Help, Commandant?"

"*Ja.*" Ludendorff tucked the flask beneath his belt and straightened himself. He looked up at Edmund seriously. "Not only *work* can set you free. The truth can do that too."

Edmund gulped.

"The head of this compound, Gotifried Harrer, has a history. It has been circulating amongst the ranks that he has lost touch with the international convention of war."

Edmund stared blankly.

"He has broken the rules, Edmund. To dispense one's infantry to their death is one thing, but to directly murder one's infantry is something else altogether. Do you know of what I speak?"

Edmund stood silent, too petrified to move a muscle.

"I have been given some intelligence that Commandant Harrer murdered a German soldier yesterday. I was also informed that *you* were present. Can you account for this, Edmund?"

All Edmund could see was the distant stare of Julius' eyes. He nodded.

"You saw this happen?"

"It happened behind me, Kommandant. I still have the soldier's blood on the back of my neck. I was ordered to bury him in the woods."

"You can account for the whereabouts of this grave?"

"*Ja, Kommandant.*"

Ludendorff nodded, rose to his feet and straightened his

coat and hat. "I will need you to testify of this incident in a trial. Tomorrow, I will return and relieve Commandant Harrer of his position. After that, I will see what I can do to secure your freedom."

Ludendorff motioned to leave.

"Commandant?"

The officer stepped back before Edmund curiously. "Speak."

"I would rather something else, Commandant."

"Pardon?" Ludendorff said with a hint of outrage.

Suddenly, Ludendorff was taken off balance slightly, displaying a sudden discomfort within him. His hand went to his chest and his head as if following a trail of pain.

"Kommandant?"

"It must be the whisky… I-I feel a warmth in me."

Ludendorff looked up at Edmund instantly.

A scratching noise.

Edmund caught the sight of a crude shadow whisk past one of the holes from the outside.

"What did you want to ask me, Edmund?"

"If my wife and daughter are alive to save, I wish you to free them in my place. They were put on the train bound for Buchenwald."

Ludendorff straightened. His hand quickly went to his belt and collected a little black book. He also withdrew a small pencil.

"Names?"

Edmund gulped.

"Fabiane Emilia Adamski. My wife."

"Age?"

"Thirty-five, Kommandant."

Edmund feasted his eyes on the swift fashion that Ludendorff pencilled his wife's beautiful name.

"And?"

"Helina Florentyna Adamski. My daughter. She is fourteen."

"Any illnesses?"

"*Nein, Kommandant.* They were healthy when last I saw them. That was over a month ago."

Ludendorff finished writing, slid the pencil back with precision, closed the book and tucked it back into his belt. He hesitated, then retrieved his silver flask and tossed it onto the bed.

"Keep it. It will keep you warm."

Ludendorff gave Edmund the slightest nod before leaving him.

The sorrowful past bound the Ettersberg Hills. Edmund stared at them at dawn and embraced hope. He chose to try and do his duty, although he had no energy. All that lurked in his stomach was the whisky. He kept the silver flask in his coat pocket along with the stale bread. He noticed activity by the front of the Headquarters. A car was leaving the gates: a long, black sedan bearing the red flags of Nazi Germany on either side of its hood. Ludendorff taking his leave, he thought. Perhaps to search for his family, among other matters.

Edmund listened to the foolish soldiers charge into the woodlands. The recent ritual of the Harrer barracks. However, something caught his attention. From the treetops nearby, things flew and swooped. Undesirable things. Dangerous things.

Trooping things.

Edmund went back into his shelter.

It didn't take him long to turn his trousers and coat inside out.

Edmund waited until he saw Ludendorff's car return. It was an hour before he had the courage to empty his wood by the rear door. He was startled by raised voices from within the Headquarters. He heard both Harrer and Ludendorff arguing. He went to a nearby window and could hear everything.

"The regional leader has condemned your actions! You have been allowed the opportunity to give yourself up for arrest!"

"You have no authority in my Headquarters!"

The intense war of political insults even drew the attention of some of the soldiers.

"I claim *seizure of power* to this compound!"

"Leave before I arrest and sentence you!"

"You swore an oath to the *Führer* to abide by the rules of war, and I—"

A single gunshot.

Then, a scatter of machine-gun fire, which came from different directions from the inside. Ludendorff had personal guards too, so that evened out the exchange. Edmund gasped. He thought fearfully if Ludendorff had the chance to search for his family.

Harrer suddenly burst out of the rear door, pistol in hand and barrel smoking. He carried a wound to his left arm.

Soldiers noticed and hesitated. Harrer then saw Edmund and his face contorted with revulsion.

"Seize him!"

Edmund was frozen with fear. Two soldiers threw him at Harrer's feet; he felt the pistol being pressed against his temple.

A scream.

Sounds of breaking glass. The barracks was under machine-gun fire.

More screams and counter attacks.

Harrer lifted his pistol and locked his eyes to his panicked infantry. Edmund could hear the creatures.

Squealing. Hissing. Swooping.

They had come.

Harrer stepped away and yelled orders to form ranks. The Unforgiving Court charged into the yard like an enormous swarm of ravens. The squealing was deafening. Edmund gripped his ears and saw many others do the same, even the Commandant. Edmund watched as soldiers were lifted from the snow and torn apart. He then looked at Harrer who was aiming his pistol at him.

He fired.

Edmund coughed as his lungs filled with blood.

Harrer stood over him and aimed at his right eye. He was suddenly gripped and clawed and his pistol dropped from his grasp. Edmund watched as claws dug into the Nazi's left ear and right eye socket. His body shook as he screamed in horror. More of the Court were upon him and they ripped at his coat and exposed his chest. His torso was then clawed and stripped of its covering to expose his white, blood-soaked ribs.

Edmund's final glances were of the Commandant's gut and throat being eaten. Edmund could hear the crunching of bone and before long, two of the Court raised the Nazi's rib cage from the foundations of his corpse and hovered it above the slaughter.

Epilogue

Weimar, Central Germany, 1987.

Erich had never been requested to take a group of visitors out this far. The memorial of Buchenwald was further north, but this group directed him onto the winding tracks to the west. They were a party of four. Erich smoked his cigarette as the cold mist slowly consumed them. He eyed the surroundings.

He'd heard of many such sites, which all were deserted like this one. The grass had not fully concealed man's intrusion over time. There were the foundations of a building and the remains of a fence boundary. Erich felt uneasy as he stared at the forest hills. He'd heard rumours that it was a haunted place. He had read enough history to know that the U.S. bombing in 1945 destroyed most of what was built for the German war effort. But there was something else about *this* site to the west. A slaughter happened, so it was written, but nothing was ever known of the cause.

The group returned from the mist and he drove them onward to the Buchenwald memorial.

An hour later Erich returned to the overgrown grasses of the site, later researched as belonging to SS Commandant Gotifried Harrer. Erich found the remains of an old iron shack. He noticed a small bunch of flowers and a note.

To my dear father, Edmund.
I understand the sacrifice you made for us.
We will love you always.
Your family, Fabiane and Helina.

A lump developed in Erich's throat.
Then, he heard something scratch at the iron.

Skewered

Long fingernails tapped at the glass, bouncing echoes off the enormous ceiling. The green vase was turned in hands like stretched leather. *Tap, tap, tap,* went the nails in examination. A dusty mist swirled within the vase, as though agitated by the tapping upon its home. The hands shook it a little. Large, yellow eyes inspected, and a deep voice said, "Hardly enough. A pitiful effort, if I must say."

"But there are at least fifty in there! That is the quota, isn't it?"

The deep voice let out a raspy laugh. "You've been away too long. The quota has changed over the years. The soul count is far greater."

The vase was tossed back, and the procurer caught it with an effort not to let it slip from his weak hands.

"One hundred. No less."

"But I want to come home! I long for the heat of our cauldrons. I'm getting too old in this mortal shell and it's too cold amongst the humans! Please, let me come—"

"One hundred souls! Now get out!"

The old demon was left to watch the fiery gates slam shut.

James paced down the side of the dark highway with his thumb out to the passing motorists. The wind was like ice to his cheeks. He regretted missing the last train out of Flinders Street, but he wore a smirk nonetheless. He'd had a great night out with the boys at Allan's buck's party. A tour of four pubs and not to mention the strip joint. Now that it was all behind him, what he needed was to get home.

He stared at the traffic as it continued to pass him by. Headlights glared into his vision every few seconds, then a large, old sedan pulled up.

James jogged up to the car, not believing his luck. The car's engine was loud and tired, and he climbed into the warm interior which smelt like old socks. The car began to move off before he could close the heavy door. He strapped on his belt, muttering a thank you, before turning to the driver.

He opened his mouth to speak, but at the sight of his saviour, found that he couldn't. The driver, an old man, looked sick. Even in the dark interior, James could make out the old man's outline, the crude shadow-puppet that sat hunched, frozen and silent.

Headlights revealed a pale and heavily-wrinkled face that hung from the skull like wet laundry. The man's hands were positioned at two and ten on the steering wheel, bony knuckles curled tightly around the rim. The fingernails looked overly long.

"Thanks for stopping," James finally said, trembling a little.

Skin folded and creased from around the edges of the driver's thin lips. James figured it to be an attempt at a grin.

"Not at all," he said; the plumbing in his throat sounded ancient.

"So, what's your name? I'm James."

"Kossloch. Some call me, Koss."

"Kozz-lok? Is that Russian or something? My old man was part Russian. Where are you from?" James said in a pitiful attempt to make small talk.

The old man turned his head slightly and said, "Not from around here."

"Ok, well thanks for giving me this ride, anyway. I need to get to Werribee. Are you heading out that far?"

"I'm going to Yarraville."

James scratched the front of his nose – that was a half hour before his place.

"Oh. There wouldn't be a chance that you could drive me out there. I'd pay you, of course. Once we get to my place."

"Don't want to drive out that far, boy."

Bugger. He had no cash left; he'd spent his last few bills on drinks. He hated getting cabs. A rip-off, but in this case, it was a cab or a hell of a long walk. He didn't fancy freezing his nuts off.

"My phone's dead, man. You wouldn't happen to have a phone at your place I could borrow?"

"You can use my landline."

"That'll be sweet, thanks."

Koss thumbed on the indicators, leading them off the Westgate Bridge and into the suburb of Yarraville. The large sedan complained at every turn. Rusted metal ground together as they snaked through the quiet streets.

The breaks squealed to a halt and a loud crank sounded

when Koss pulled up the hand break. The engine died in a symphony of clunking and rattling. Koss, saying nothing, opened his door and struggled out into the cold. James did the same.

He followed Koss up a small gravel path. Koss was shorter than he'd imagined, and walked as if his back carried a hump. The house had its lights on, and Koss stood before the door beneath the amber glow of the porch light. He produced a wrinkly grin, revealing a set of yellow and brown teeth and said, "Go on in." He presented a bony hand to the door and pushed it open into an empty, lit hallway. "The phone is down the hall."

"Thanks."

James stepped across the threshold when a bony hand pressed into the centre of his back.

The door slammed shut.

He turned but Koss was no longer there. When James turned back to the hall, his heart froze.

At the far end, a woman in a white dress emerged. She was tall, with a head of shaggy brown hair. Her face was long, wrinkled and she looked at him curiously, longingly even. Others began to silently show themselves from behind her. A mix of men and women. Fat and thin. All staring. All dressed in loose clothing that looked to have not seen their laundry day in months.

James took a small step backward, snapping his gaze at all before him in turn.

The woman's white dress was covered in an obscure pattern of smeared colours – reds, dark purples and browns. Her gaze was fixed on him, looking him up and down. The edges of her thick purple lips curled into a small grin and she nodded. "He will do, I guess. A lean offering, but tall. However. . . how to have him?" she said.

What the hell was she talking about—

Something sharp pierced his back.

Someone *was* behind him.

He turned his head. Knees shaking. Eyes watering. A stinging, burning pain surged through his abdomen. Blood rose in his throat and dripped out of the corners of his mouth. An obese man, bald and wearing nothing but a bloodied white singlet, pulled a long blade from James' body. *A sword?*

Koss was present now.

"Are there any others?" the woman said.

"Give me a break, you greedy bitch. You'll have to make do with him tonight," Koss said as though every word was a struggle. "Just get it over with so I can collect it."

James looked on with watering eyes; a green vase was held tight in Koss' hands.

The tip of the blood-coated blade was pressed into the soft meat of James' shoulder, and then forced all the way down, piercing lung, stomach and intestines.

Kossloch reaped the green essence of the soul into his vase as the body bled out. He sealed the opening with a cork. The clan were onto the body before he'd closed the front door behind him.

When he was outside once more, he stared at his vase of the damned. He shivered within the mortal shell, longing for the thick, hot scales of his natural form.

He needed to make it back home.

"Only forty-eight more, and this 'meals-on-wheels' shit will be over. I just have to survive and endure. Survive and endure," he said aloud, as from the house, the woman's voice squealed with delight. "Like a kid in a candy store."

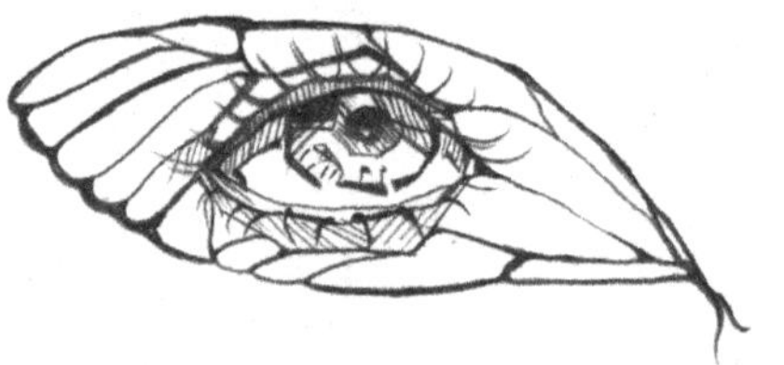

The Reconstruction of Melissa

Melissa wished that she could slice the middle age off her face with a razor. To drag the point of the steel across her jaw line and pull off the façade rejected by men she desired. Then, she could replace it with something men would stop at nothing to have. This fantasy lingered in the pit of her stomach, even when she slept. This dream placed her in a weird and wonderful room with a lavish tall ceiling, an open fireplace and exposed beams. The surroundings were filled with a gathering of people and the buzz of conversation like bees in a hive.

The lighting was warm, and classical music lingered with the familiar scratching of a gramophone. Through the crowd of faces that drifted by in a smear of colour, she noticed Jacob. He was smartly clad in a navy-blue club blazer and sipping at a glass of liquor. Jacob was young and handsome, but showed no interest in her. So she thought of razors.

As she slipped into the depths of the murmuring sea, she lost sight of Jacob after an exclamation broke from the crowd. A man entered wearing a surgical mask and pushing a small trolley. The party focused on him eagerly, their eyes wide with anticipation. When he stopped, they gasped with excitement when he lifted a silver dome from his trolley and presented them with an unknown gift.

He was serving something; handing it out piece by piece

with hands that were fitted with white surgical gloves that gradually developed red and brown stains the more he handled the offering. The closer Melissa got, the more she could see what he donated.

It was raw meat, and everyone who'd received their share was feasting on it, dribbling its juices from their mouths.

He caught sight of her as she watched with bewilderment and removed his mask. He was an aged man, experience shining in his eyes, and he was smiling. He held out a larger portion and dangled it as if to tempt her. It showed traces of pale pigments – was it skin? With every passing second, her eyes ate at what he held.

She gasped and stumbled backward, knocking into some of the guests. Her gaze caught her reflection in a crystal wine glass – her white eyes within a red canvas. The music stopped abruptly, and all attention was brought to her. Everyone paused, their faces now white and grimacing. Some inched away nervously at the sight of her. Others dry retched. She looked on in horror at what he held.

It was a face.

Her face.

Startled from her troubled sleep, Melissa squinted at the intense light. She shielded her eyes with her forearm for a few moments to allow the sting in her pupils to subside. The brilliance was coming from a large pair of glass doors to her left. Thin white drapes danced lazily on a salty breeze.

She was in a bed, comfortable and enormous. A single

silk sheet draped over her. The rest of the room was white and still. A single armchair rested in the corner by the window, and a closed door with a gold knob was to her right. Then she noticed him – the man with the trolley…

He was sitting at her bedside, watching and waiting.

She gasped at the sight of him, and then realized that her head was bandaged. Her hands drifted up to her face, and the more she felt the wrapping, the more her dread deepened. She pulled and clawed at the bandages that mummified her.

He leapt up and pushed her hands away. "Stop it! Calm down!"

She tried to talk only to find that she couldn't. Her tongue felt numb and so she mumbled with terror.

"Easy! Please, Melissa! You must not stress your face!"

She scratched at him, kicking out and dislodging the silk sheet. She was wearing a satin gown and her legs were bare. As her gown's tie was loosened and slipped away through her panic, she caught sight of her panties. They were white and laced. They were not hers…

Where was she? What had happened? Was the gathering in the weird and wonderful room a nightmare? Was this a new delirium? She mumbled, tried to scream, but was helpless beneath the man's strength.

She felt a sharp pain to her arm and looked wildly at him as he pressed the plunger of a syringe. It took only a second or two before heavy weights within her chest began to pull her down.

The second after that, black.

Her tongue was dry and her throat craved moisture. Slowly, her eyes opened. She blinked. Darkness. Silence. Was she finally awake? Really? Was everything a nightmare? Was she back home in her apartment? If she was, then no doubt her cat Pebbles would be asleep near her feet. As she began to wake fully, she allowed her feet to wander in search of the warm lump that Pebbles would be when he was slumbering.

He wasn't there.

"Melissa? Do you remember where you are? Who *I* am?"

Her heart was in her mouth. No nightmare. She could scream now. Strength was returning. She heard his voice beneath her terror, but it was distant. His hands gripped her shoulders and she fought him. She swung out at him. She screamed.

Soon, the sharp pain again, then the weights.

Black.

Her arms and legs were tied to the bed when she woke. This time, she decided not to fight. There were no illusions. Everything was happening. This was real. Her head felt clouded and heavy and her eyes rolled uncontrollably – no doubt due to the effects of the drugs he'd pumped into her. She couldn't take another dose of whatever he would stab into her every rebellion. No. This time, she lay on the bed and remained silent and waited to be awake fully.

"Are you going to relax this time?" he asked from the bedside.

Silence.

"If you promise to act civilized, then I will untie you. I just can't risk you harming yourself. You must understand this… you can talk, Melissa. Your voice should be operable by now. The effects of the sedation would have worn off hours ago. Say something."

Melissa took some time and swirled her tongue. She had moisture and was able to draw her voice forth. "What do you want from me?" she muttered.

"To wake up!" he laughed. "To be honest, you've been in that bed for five days. You've come in and out of delirious dreams, but that is to be expected through all the sedation. Your dreams would have been rather strange, I would imagine? I feel it is time now to swing you back into reality. Piece by piece… You have soiled the sheets four times in your sleep. So, in turn I have changed you and the bed…"

She bit at her tongue as her heart began to race; the mere thought of this man handling her when she was naked and unconscious simply ate at her marrow. "Untie me," she wheezed.

"So I won't need this, then?" he asked as he held out a syringe.

"No."

He stepped around the bed and undid the ropes, and she slowly sat up. He motioned to place a pillow behind her back, but she cowered immediately, gasping, "Don't touch me!"

"Settle down," he said before taking his seat. "This is getting tedious, Melissa. For someone who could sustain so much suffering, you are, surprisingly, a drama queen."

She eyed him wildly as her memory had begun to focus.

With every recollected image, the more she would inch from him with dread. Who he was. Where he had her… what he did. She remembered his haunting breaths as he cut into her face. His fingers probing her tissue and clamping it, turning it… tucking it.

"You monster…" she whimpered with tears welling in her eyes.

"You lasted almost two hours into the procedure. I was impressed. You even would have felt the beginnings of the bone reconstruction before you finally passed out."

Melissa's tears began to flow.

"There, there. Understand this, to become a masterpiece, you need to earn it. Perfection comes at a price, Melissa."

"You tortured me!"

"Some other surgeons have intercourse with their patients whilst they lie in a limp sleep. I know of others that even discretely slice off a souvenir, for instance, a tiny portion of musculature, a nip of flesh from the back of the ear. But me? I just have a fetish for watching people suffer… You'll forgive me like the others have."

"What did you do to me?" she cried as she shielded herself with the satin gown.

"Let me assure you, Melissa, that you have not been violated. I have taken good care of you, both during and after the operation. I've undressed and bathed you, delicately placing you in my large warm spa. Cleaning you as I cradled you in my arms. Drying you slowly, and dressing you in the finest satin and silk… I've treated you like a china doll, with the utmost care and devotion."

"You!… Sick!… Fu—"

"How about we take in some fresh air?" he said as he rose from his chair and held out a hand. "Come, you have a balcony outside. It is just past midday, so you haven't missed the sun this time."

She remained frozen for a few moments, but he did not move. Apart from her remembering what he'd done to her, the rest of his identity remained in shadow. He leaned towards her with his hand out, waiting. She didn't want to touch him. The dizziness swirled within her bandaged head and terror filled her with thoughts of what he might do if she didn't do as he asked. She raised her trembling hand and he grabbed it, giving her no chance to hesitate.

He led her slowly across the brightly-lit bedroom and towards the large glass doors. Her steps were heavy, and her knees shook as they struggled to maintain her weight. He helped her with a gentle hand at her lower back and a supporting grip on her left arm.

Surrounded by a white railing, the paved balcony was graced with a small table and two chairs. Spread across the table was what appeared to be a breakfast setting. There was silverware containing milk, a fruit platter, and orange juice. The outside world forced her to squint but her eyes soon adjusted. The balcony faced toward a beautiful view of a yellow beach and a blue ocean. She could see surfers riding the distant breaks, and although they were too far away to hear her calls if she were to cry out, just seeing other inhabitants comforted her somewhat. He led her to the table and pulled out a chair.

"Sit."

She did so, and a helping of oatmeal rested before her.

Silver cutlery was placed precisely on either side of her service, and a modest selection of Danish pastries were stacked on a white porcelain plate.

"You must be famished," he said. "Eat something. Regrettably, the oatmeal will be cold, but I could have it warmed if you wish."

She rejected instantly with a shake of her head and stared at the table. Her heart was beating so hard she could feel her ears thump to its rhythm.

What is all of this?

"It is important that you get nourished, Melissa. It would help work the muscles of your cheeks… Aren't you going to eat anything?"

"Why?"

"Why what?"

"Why don't you just kill me? Get it over with? Enough games… just do it…"

He laughed merrily. "My dear, I am no killer. What fun would there be in that? None for me I'm afraid. You are right in the sense of the probable ease of it all. It would be simple. I *could* slit your throat, but what for? Tossing you aside would be like Picasso destroying one of his works of art. My methods of practice are usually confused with thoughts that I am out to murder, which is untrue. It is understandable for you to fear such things but try to relax."

"What did you do to my face?"

"What you asked me to do. You still don't remember?"

Her head swam.

"I performed a Rhytidectomy and a Rhinoplasty for you."

She stared at him blankly, struggling to keep her head

straight.

"A face lift and a nose job?" he prompted.

"I-I don't believe you..." she wept.

"There, there. You will see. Your memory will awaken before long, and it will tell you that you didn't need to fly to places like Argentina, India, and Cuba to receive what I have given you for half the price. Overseas, the importance of post-surgery support is often overlooked and regrettably, the risk of complications is high. But not here. Not with me. But enough of that for now. You must eat. Even just a little bit. You need to regain some of your energy."

She sat silent, thinking of the horror that would be reflected when she finally looked into a mirror. What did this sicko do to her? Did he turn her nose inside out? Make her flesh mimic the distortion of Picasso's paintings? The *'Weeping Woman'* image suddenly entered her mind – the fat lips, the disproportioned features, the dark colours of the skin... What did he do? What *was* beauty in the mind of this deranged pervert?

She picked up her silver spoon in her quivering hand but couldn't bring herself to do anymore. She trembled with every laboured movement, holding back tears of bewilderment; she couldn't even place within her mind where she could have met such a man. How did she come to be in his keeping? Perhaps time would reveal such answers, and that scared her even more... She let the spoon fall from her grasp.

"You don't want to eat, my dear?" he said before placing a hand behind her neck and tightened his grip. Melissa tried to shake him off but her strength had not fully returned and so he held her in place.

"Understand this. I only care about my work. Your face has had hours of my skill devoted to it, and your ignorance is endangering the finish," he said as he gathered the silver spoon and scooped up a portion of the cold oatmeal.

"I don't care about the rest of you. Your arms, your legs. If you choose to disrespect my art, then I will happily remove the portions of skin from behind your knees and stand you in a pool of salt water. I would enjoy that, you know. I could hear you scream for days." He smirked as he raised the spoon to her lips, tightening his grip on her neck until her trembling lips opened.

"That's better," he said as he fed her. "You made the right choice for yourself."

The sun had descended into the later part of the afternoon when he led her back inside. He sat her before a large oval mirror and began to slowly undo the bandages around her head.

She sat as still as she could. She was petrified, listening to his murmurs as he unwound the white cloths. The pressure that the bounds had applied loosened as they were removed, and tingles of pain broke out on her skin. "Let's see how we went here?" he said through gritted teeth. "Just a few more layers and we are there…"

A cold sweat covered her as more of her memory began to seep in. She could hear the voices of her friends in her head. "We know of someone!" the voices echoed, but she could not retain the relevance.

She sat on her hands and closed her eyes. The bandages

were gone, and he sighed a breath of accomplishment. She bit at her lip and refused to look.

What horror had he unleashed upon her face? What monstrosity did he turn her into? Her fear could only make her conjure up the worst.

"Open your eyes…" he whispered in her ear, and the sudden closeness forced her to yelp.

"Open them…" he whispered again, but with a bit more force this time.

She shook her head and began to cry.

"Open… just take a peek."

"I'll scream! I'll scream until someone hears me! I'll scream until you cut out my tongue, you sick—"

"Look!" he yelled as he clamped the back of her neck with a strong hand and shook her enough to break the tight seal of her eyelids. She turned her head furiously but again, he was too strong. He gripped her chin to keep her steady before the mirror.

"Just look!" he yelled, growing tired of her stubbornness. Her vision was a blur through her tears, but she forced herself to look, she had to – what choice did she have?

She looked upon her reflection, blinking to clear her vision.

Melissa gasped at the sight.

"What did I tell you?" he asked quietly.

Her hand slowly raised, trembling fingers gliding over her jaw. She directed her wild eyes to him through the mirror. "I don't understand," she whispered as her fingers continued to explore the perfect curves – she looked as she did when she was twenty-one. . . maybe even younger.

"Now, can you remember why you came to me?"

"No…" she gasped; not a single wrinkle was present. Nothing.

"Let me help you," he began as he knelt beside her and looked at her through the mirror as she was lost to the wonder of her new façade. "You look young, vibrant, and seductive. You are no longer the aging prune. Remember what you told me… before the procedure?"

"Jacob…" she suddenly recalled.

"That's right. You've longed for him. Hungered for him, yet his eyes are only for that of his wife. His *young* wife. You have what you want now, Melissa. You are armed with the beauty to seduce him. Isn't that what you wanted? You may be middle-aged, but you are still the same naughty little lady that destroys marriages and families."

She turned her head to him wildly.

"I've studied you, Melissa. You have an impressive history. Ten years ago, you drove a woman to insanity and she cut off her husband's genitals. Marriage after marriage you destroyed as you worked your way from one rich duke to the next… Of course, your dirty business went dry when your face finally caught up to your age. Nothing would work anymore, would it? Your failed attempts upon Jacob – or any other man for that matter – drove you to me."

She stared at her new beauty; it was hypnotizing.

"We have both achieved what we wanted through this, haven't we? I have heard the delightful sounds of your suffering, and you? You have regained your armour, the main tool of your trade."

"He will love this, won't he?" she whispered.

"Not only him, but the men that will obviously follow. Knowing your pattern."

She laughed nervously, and it hurt.

"However, I am not sure how Jacob's young wife would cope with your sabotage upon their union. I believe she suffers from depression."

"I don't care about her."

"I guess it is onward for you, then."

"When can I leave here?"

"You are fit to leave when you wish, everything you had on when you came here is neatly folded in the dresser. The keys to your car are by the bed."

"So, I can go?"

"Yes, you paid me in advance," he began as he rose. "Although, I think it is best for you to remain here for at least a day or so, perhaps even through the weekend? I have a heated pool down stairs, a paid chef, and I could have a manicurist and masseur here within the hour to tend to your every need. Please, do not go so hastily. Not while I finally have you awake and able to engage in conversation. Besides, the more your face rests, the better."

"Is it Saturday tomorrow?"

"Yes."

"I want to leave, Doctor," Melissa said as she rose from the chair; she was still terrified of him. She back stepped to the dresser to collect her clothes.

"Why must you leave? The fun doesn't have to end now, you know."

"You have already had your fun with me."

"Indeed I have."

"I can live with that, Doctor, but I must go. It is onward for me, you said that before."

"Ah, an opportunity to see Jacob, I gather?"

"A country club dinner," she continued as she laid out her clothes on the bed, keeping a nervous eye on him the whole time.

"I see."

"If you would excuse me, Doctor," she said, and this time a smile rose to her lips. "You've had *your* fun, now it's time I had mine."

MY CLAIRE

Anyone else would think it was a miracle. To have a loved one return to you. Sure, I admit I was happy to see her, hoping her death had been some horrible mistake. Perhaps she didn't get drunk that night with her friends and go swimming in that river. Maybe Claire didn't drown. The current could've taken her far down stream, you know, beyond the span of the search party. It's not unheard of that people can grab a floating log and keep their head above water, is it? I wasn't a fool to be so optimistic. That's what sprang to mind when she rapped on my door in the late hours, saying, "Poppy, I'm back!"

However, my Claire is not a miracle.

She's just another of the Lost who won't rest.

"Hold still!" I said through gritted teeth.

"It hurts."

"That's just confusing. How the bloody hell can anything hurt you?"

With a final tug, the axe came free from its wedge of brain and bone. I set the bloodied tool down and held back the urge to retch; blobs of brain matter clung to the blade and glistened eerily in the firelight. The smell was worse, believe it or not. Imagine rotting fish mixed with mouldy cheese, and you would see what I mean.

Bile rose in my throat as she fingered the split in her head. "Would you stop doing that? You're making me sick!"

"Can you stitch it up for me?" she asked.

Her eyes, although cataract-grey, still somehow held that glimmer of her former self. She'd been a cheeky teenager and had always managed to get me to do things with that look of hers. I fool you not; there was a time she had me out with my rifle one cold night to check there were no intruders trying to pry open her window. She was good to be nervous. It made her careful; after all, she'd inherited her late mother's good looks—pity her nerves never told her that booze and swimming didn't go together.

"Stitches? What good will that do you? It won't heal. You should've listened to me and stayed in the barn!"

"Is that it for me then, Poppy? I'm just to stay out there? Why can't I stay in the house with you?"

The funny thing was, even though she was dead, she was still as sensitive a soul as ever. I didn't have the heart to tell her that she reeked. When she'd first arrived, the decomposition had yet to reveal the yellowing pus that dripped from her nose. Her greening, peeling skin, the bloating that had formed in her neck, and of course, the decay shrinking her cheeks.

"It's safer for you out there, you know, in case people come knocking." I sighed and washed my hands at the sink, watching the blood dilute across the day-old dishes; she always used to do them for me.

"Are you mad at me, Poppy?" she asked, sitting up from

the kitchen table.

"Good guess. It's not every day one's granddaughter is waiting for you when you return from ploughing the fields, with an axe wedged in her skull. You're lucky the bastard didn't take your head off!" I said as I spun and locked eyes with her. "Did anyone see you? Do I have to ready my rifle?"

"No, it was just him. He was alone, you see. Working on that nice car of his."

"You stupid girl," I hissed.

"I'm sorry, Poppy. I couldn't help it. I could smell him a mile away!"

"That's the minister's son out there! Sprawled in the mud with a gaping hole in his neck! You know the law: *'If the dead return, bring them now to burn'*." I raked fingers through my thinning, grey hair and nodded. "If the townsfolk find out I kept you; they'll burn us both. Together, in Main Street, as an example. It's tradition they still hold to now. Didn't you learn anything in school?"

"I'm sorry, Poppy…"

I sighed. "Why did you have to do it? Why run the risk of exposing us?"

She shrugged, scratching the back of her decaying neck. "I was hungry, Poppy."

"I told you to feast on my sheep and cattle."

"It's not the same. They're like bad milk to me, not like—" She turned a longing gaze to the back door, obviously yearning for the Minister's son's carcass, waiting for her in the mud. "—like him."

"I'm going to throw up…" I faced away from her, took deep, calming breaths before turning back. "Where's the granddaughter I use to love? That's why I couldn't let the mob find you."

"She died in the river. You know that. But Poppy, I'm still here. It's still me. I'm just different, is all. I promise I'll try and be good."

"But you won't change."

"I wish I could, but I can't. Only now, I understand why all others like me couldn't change. They have no real choice; the hunger just won't go away."

"Well, you better get to it then," I said, turning away from her and resting both hands on the sink.

"Does that mean I can keep him?"

"Evidence is in my backyard, so yes, you get to keep him. But, on one condition."

"Anything, Poppy."

"You eat everything. Right down to the bones. There must not be anything left to find. Got it?"

"Yes, Poppy," she said, making for the back door.

"Claire?"

She snapped a look at me; the hunger in her grey eyes reflected the emerging monster—the thing that would remain, leaving no trace of the granddaughter I loved.

"The town will be searching for that lad. You're never to leave that barn again, okay?"

"What about my next meal?" she said in a voice deeper than normal. A drop of thick drool fell from the corner of her mouth. A mouth that commonly enjoyed a coat of pink lipstick, only then to resort to flaky skin and darkening ulcers.

My mouth went dry. "D-don't worry about that. Go and

have your dinner."

I watched her drag the minister's son to the barn, the grunt of her exertion carried through to the kitchen window like a sickly gasp of a starving wolf.

She feasted for hours.

Every crunch of bone was like a nail in my heart. With each tear of flesh, images flooded of snapping teeth digging into raw meat; cracks forming in the once-perfect picture I had of her.

There was enough time for me to chain the barn doors.

To pour the fuel.

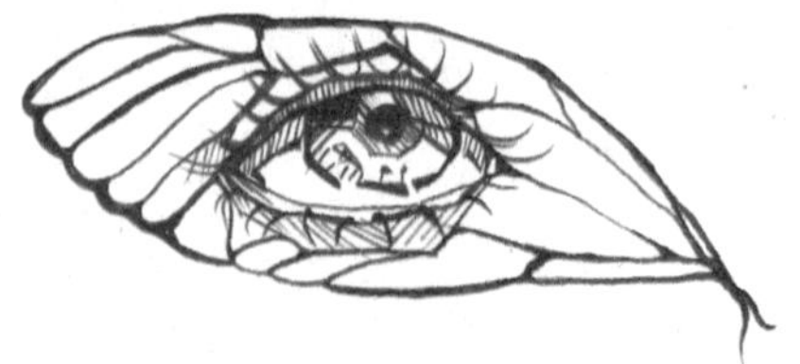

Sister of Charity

Anna cried as she ran.

The night's chill clung to her cheeks. Her knuckles were red and raw, the feeling of the face they'd beaten still fresh in their memory.

She gasped at the sight of the orphanage, its gates tall and welcoming. Looking over both shoulders, heart hammering, she slid through a hole in the fence; a secret she'd known well as a child.

It was past midnight. There were no lights on in the main building. A few security lamps glowed, but she had no problems avoiding their sights as she staggered through the graveyard, nearly breathless.

Anna yanked her long coat free from the thorns of a rose bush. The clack of her flat-heeled shoes upon the pathway sent an echo, as though ghosts' teeth were chattering around her. Fatigued, she leaned on the door of the cottage.

Knock. Knock.

Heavy footsteps shuffled from within and she heard the chink of keys. Anna concealed her bloodied hands beneath her coat.

The door opened with a squeal. Before her was Sister Rionach; the old nun who'd helped raise her.

"My dear! Is that really you?" she said, peering at her from the only eye that worked. The other, Anna remembered, was a vacant, pale orb.

"Sister!" Anna cried. "Something terrible has happened!"

"Now, now, you come inside and get out of the cold."

The small cottage was warm, and the lighting was deep with amber. The shadows were black and the air thick with the scent of old clothes; smoke dwindled from a small pot-belly oven. An iron jug of tea was brewing. Sister Rionach ushered her to sit upon the single bed, dragging over a small stool to sit beside her.

Sister Rionach eased down with a grunt. The years had not been kind to her; more lines dragged down her cheeks and her back carried a larger hump. She still wore a black gown, and a cornette headpiece of white cloth, folded upwards, resembling butterfly wings.

"Now, child, tell me what happened?"

"I have sinned, Sister. I have brought someone to harm. Her name is Elizabeth, and I have hurt her."

"Who is she, dear?"

"A dancer at my school," she said, the slender face she'd broken flashing into her mind.

"You dance? Like an angel, I'm sure."

"Elizabeth is better... I want what she has. She has more grace, nicer dresses, better parents."

"Oh, my dear. You were adopted by good people, too. A banker and his wife. She was a seamstress? Did they not provide for you?"

"Yes, but Elizabeth has a better life."

"Don't hide."

"Pardon, Sister?"

"Your little hands," said Sister Rionach. "Let me see them."

Anna hesitated. The blood was sticky between her fingers. She eased them out, and her heart quickened. Sister Rionach's face knotted.

"Is she dead? I cannot cure you from the ultimate sin."

"No. She's alive. I'm sure of it. She was screaming curses. I deserve them."

"There, there, child."

They embraced. Anna felt comforted, even though her shoulders still burned with guilt.

"I can cure you of this sin."

"Was it my wrath?"

"No. You were brutal, yes, but you are guilty of Envy."

Sister Rionach rose from her stool and poured a cup of tea. "Drink."

Anna took a few sips.

"Now, sleep, pretty one. Tomorrow is a new dawn, and you will be cured."

Anna eased back onto the soft pillow, her head heavier with every passing second. Sighing profoundly, she drifted into slumber.

Anna woke with a gentle yawn. Her body was coated with a sprinkle of sunlight.

"Good morning. Rise, my dear."

She did, a little dazed, dizzy, still trying to wake up. She yawned again, and a stinging pain struck like a spike to her temple.

She screamed.

"Settle child! Just breathe. Let me read to you from the Gospel, like I did when you were young. It will soothe your spirit."

"What's happening?"

"I have cured you of the Envy. Never again will you look upon Elizabeth with bitterness."

Anna tried to open her eyes but couldn't.

They were no longer there.

The Soul Knows

I had seen my own death.

It played out in my head as I sat before the television. My wife, Jean, was lounging at my side. We were watching random stations; channel surfing, you might say. As the shows flashed by, my chest tightened as I stared up at the glare of the screen. I didn't think much of it at first, but as muscles and tissue continued to pulse, something was different. My phone was on my lap; it was never far away. I liked to check my social status regularly, especially when I'd posted about one my books. I'm a writer, you see. Well, trying to be one anyway.

Yes, something was odd behind the walls of my ribs. I re-adjusted myself into the cushions of the couch to ease the pinch, the inner din.

It didn't work.

I scrolled my feed as a distraction. Jean was unaware of what I was feeling whilst she worked the remote. My gaze switched between the television to my small phone screen, wishing for the unpleasantries within me to ease. To my relief, they did. I didn't even care that my earlier promotional post had gotten no interest.

No likes.

No shares.

No comments.

Zippo…

I remembered giving a slight shrug of indifference, where normally I would be agitated, sometimes to the point of tossing my phone onto the floor.

Alive to write another day.

The evening was becoming colder, and my legs felt the chill; I'd been in jean shorts for most of that day, so the drop in temperature was all the encouragement I needed to change into tracksuit pants.

That's when the vision started.

I watched it all happen in cold, sweaty detail.

As I sat there beside Jean, I watched myself walk into the bedroom and dig out some pants from my dresser. There was no warning. I watched myself collapse, drop, like a puppet would when its master would let go of its strings.

Thud!

Dead.

So instant and final.

The vision revealed Jean running to me. She dropped to her knees and rolled my body over, screaming. Jean knew I was gone. She pelted her fists onto my chest, as though angry that I'd left her so suddenly.

It's weird how visions like that can happen.

How your soul warns you, plays things out.

Jean had settled on a show. Some older film with Kevin Kline. *My Old Lady*, I think it was…

I felt fear then. Not liking the movie my mind screened before my open eyes. I inched closer to Jean, not ready to leave her or anything around us.

"Want to finish that fudge?" Jean asked.

My death played out again. Clear as anything else before me. That time I was getting out the dog food to feed my sleepy greyhound. I unzipped the large bag of pellets and dug out two scoops.

One.

Two.

Smack!

The deafening clang of the metal food dish upon the slate floor. My still body. Jean's screams…

I shuddered.

"You can have it, love," I said, rubbing my thudding chest. "I'm going to cut down on the sweets."

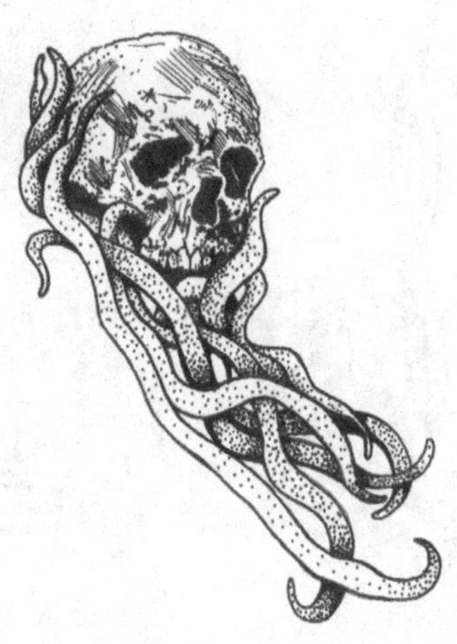

CREEPING SKELETONS

Weird Poetics of Fantasy and Horror

Beneath the Ferny Trees

My grandma, when a little girl,
One gloomy, storm-cloud night,
Ran up the path around her house
To see a dreadful sight;
Among the twisted, ferny trees
In shadows dense and black,
A gathering of terrors lurked
Around a moving sack.
Foul lights lit out from their great eyes,
A glowing, red and bright,
Brought forth the sack—released the prize,
To slay with great delight.
And I then saw the feasting beasts—
"The horror!" Grandma cried.
So off I ran back to the house
Beneath my bed to hide.
My ears could hear the distant screams,
And many tears were shed.
I cried in mourning for that soul,
Devoured by the dead.

The Realm of Angels

The raging skies above us reach
A cracking thunder of the night;
I press my feet upon this beach,
The coldest wind, it brings a bite.

So slowly now I draw quite near,
My student with the golden wings,
I lean to her, "What's wrong my dear?"
From her full brightened lips, she sings:

I travel'd down to Earth's fair ground,
When fire burned and humans cried,
The screams, the terror; what a sound,
I ask you now: why must some die?

I flew through burning wood and stone,
I carried bodies; pain had come,
The flames were fierce; one died alone,
Not all were saved, oh only some…

My fingers stroke her gentle face,
Her tears stream down, so thick, so red,
I say to her, "Rest in this place,
And not dwell on the ones left dead.

"This world of shores and endless sea,
Was forged for angels for their rest,
The sacred sands let us be free,
From toils that put us to the test.

"For here we sleep; we take a breath,
The clouds glow white or fill with rain,
For days, for years, we hide from Death,
To rescue humans from its pain.

"When angels travel far and down
To interrupt in Death's foul schemes,
We try our best; we do not frown,
If some slip through into saddest dreams."

Note of the Executioner

I break the slabs. Halving that oak,
They fall—so splintered—at my feet.
I fetch another: I'm not beat,
I wipe my sweat upon my cloak.

I bring fresh water to my stone,
By day, by night, my axe is sharp.
I rest my axe, I play my harp,
I train, I slumber on my own.

I walk to work on paths so long,
To carry out my chopping task.
The days I wear the plain black mask,
I hear their breaths—foreboding song.

Some cower, crying with repent!
The others fight and curse the crown,
Until their necks are fastened down.
My axe holds death—and they are sent.

I venture home holding my pay,
My duty now until I'm old.
My leather pouch holds shiny gold,
For lopping noggins every day.

The Torturer's Oath

Come with me, dear Sir, simply follow my voice,
The blindfold leaves you shrouded in mystery,
Bereft of sight and choice,
Enter my chamber, my secret place, a domain of
eternal sin,
Allow me to uncover your eyes, sit you down,
Now we must begin.

Forgive the dimness of this room,
I will light a candle and present my tools,
Look here!
See numerous implements fit for surgeons,
And where you sit – 'tis my loyal stool.

Let me fasten your shins and wrists,
Notch by notch – strong and tight,
Draw your fearful eyes to my dear friend at your feet,
My hungry and rusted vice!

Questions shall come later, so silence your tongue,
'tis my advice,
You dealt in business that made me look the fool,
So for that, dear Sir,
You must first pay the price.

See my rusted, crimson friend,
Its metal lips hungry and wide,
Let me secure your right foot behind its teeth,
Press in the bolted clamps at its side.

I turn the lever, slow and sure,
Allowing your shin to burn red as a rose,
Yes, I hear your screams – the tearing; the *crunch*!
I shall not stop until the metal lips close.

There now, draw your breath,
Your dues are surely paid,
You must see the result of your suffering,
Let us look down at what we have made.

Allow me to assist you forward,
Guide your head against your will,
Let me loosen the brace, shift your leg,
For beyond the cold lips – 'tis your foot, limp and still.

We are far from anywhere, you and I,
Through twisted wood and hidden trail,
You can scream all you wish,
It will be but an echo through this secret dale.

I found your letters to my wife,
Episodes of passion and clandestine cheers,

I have read every one of them; I would have you know,
They dated back for years.

But, you see, Leonard,
I care not for this pitiful affair –
Ethel has packed and left!
There is a sudden absence to my wealth;
I know I am the victim of a filthy theft!

So, disclose to me now: where is dear Ethel?
Give her up, you gallant fool!
Or I shall unleash every craft in my chamber,
And dissect you in my stool!

Ah, the valley, you say? With a river nearby?
'Twas the manor where we were wed,
Little does she know: What I do now, I did back then,
I forged that house long before our union was said.

For in the south wing – beneath the stairs,
Lives a deep passage through a catacomb or two,
There dwells a chamber just like this,
Where I shall question Ethel, just as I have done you.

The Lord that Reigns Alone

'Tis my home beneath a veil of dust,
Desolate and snowless,
Volcanic craters like hungry mouths,
I live alone and forgotten -- powerless.
The vast lakes I once knew
Now fathomless gulfs – barren and dry,
Depths of sullen blackness and ashen air,
I am bereft of moisture to cry.
For aeons I have stared upon my crumbled throne,
Remains of my sweet queen, dearest and dead,
The bones of my kindred, the men that were,
Lay rotten in my land from feet to head.
I wander amongst the swirling sand,
My eyes dim and blind,
Yet a dense shadow desolate to the sun,
Cast by a gigantean of stone – I gasp to find.
The towering mass of enormous heights,
Its peak shrouded by angry clouds,
My mind feels the subtle hope – salvation?
Since been lost beneath an eternal shroud.
I mount the rough and cracked stone,
Climbing for the summit, battling biting cold,
Endless hours through dregs of darkness
and blinding light,

I hunger for the freedom through the gates of old.
Through my difficult ascent, I am left weak
and stranded,
With the sullen black world beneath,
I stare vertically for hours, fingers buried
in the cracks,
My slightest hope is but grey with grief.
I am dry and brittle, leather on bones,
My every joint brings an agonising sting,
I need life force – mortal blood,
Only that warm thick nectar could revive *this* king!
I summon to the heights, the mortal kingdom,
From a fallen Lord who reigns alone,
My final breath, its seductive haze,
I need but one touch upon this stone.
But, ah, the lovely allure forces a mortal hand,
Their light caress to turn their face pale,
Their blood falls the deep descent,
I press closer in eagerness so the river shalt not fail.
Through my dry veins travels the warm savage juice,
My accent is quick and cunning,
I roar to the great heights above,
"Beware for I am a-coming!"
'Twas my home that bore lanterns of light,
'Til the skin-clad savages came and began their fight,
Raging their war, their swords blood-drenched,
Turning us voiceless, lifeless, and death-clenched.

My sudden eruption into their skies,
Soaring, a-crying
With thunderbolts through my hands,
I shall be the dark deliverer
Never night nor day disturb,
Laying my brutal vengeance upon these lands.

Fateshifter

I

The Severed Kingdom

I woke in darkness, screaming at my birth,
Upon the rocky landscapes of this earth,
My realm is cloaked from all the human eyes,
In which stare blankly up towards the skies.

Upon this peak I've grown to greatest height,
My fleece that glows and horrid fists of might!
With flaming eyes and longest jaws of woe,
Observing all the ages, come and go.

So we are hidden from the mortal world,
Observing all their destinies unfurled,
Such savagery—at times—the mortals give,
They're butchering a world that we both live.

To heart, we feel the drop of destruction,
I heard my kingdom scream, "*Oblivion!*"
I'm tired of these self-destroying souls,
I see their greed, their leaders have no goals.

The mortal judgments lasted far too long,
Our realm, it cries our great foreboding song,
The skies will open doorways to their world,
And humans stare at maelstroms, full and swirled.

My monstrous kindred, hungry and deployed,
Mankind must listen, 'else shall be destroyed!

II

Lord of the Unseen World

I rest upon my mountain's peak,
To this foul Gorgon I now speak,
I pin him—screaming—with my talon's blight,
Within my kingdom; fear of me burns bright.

I torture this foul creature from the south,
Embedding nails—pulling teeth from mouth,
"Oh please!" it begs, it cries some woeful tears,
I laugh, rejoicing: I'm the sum of fears.

For tucked beneath my leather belt and straps,
All wound with coils are my precious maps,
They chart all ages of the universe,
These rolled-up, treasured parchments, how I nurse.

The knowledge is my wealth, it's truly mine,
The hidden mysteries of space and time,
My sight has reached dimensions far and wide,
It pierces far, no other world can hide.

"There's treachery!" the Gorgon cries and sways,
He bleeds the blackest blood and drools and preys,
I learned that Fateshifters that breath my air,
They plot to steal my maps; I pace and flair!

I roar, "Reveal the names and give them light!"
I find them out, they cower 'neath my sight,
Our mountains, caverns, finally see a war,
My traitors now surrender to my law!

So now they've learned, they hide and
fear withdread,
I am their Lord: respect or soon be dead.

Nosferatu

Shadows drape my mind of late,
As I walk through tainted lands,
'Tis my absent, demon state,
Forcing out my shaking hands.

How I gaze at crimson skies,
Raised through darkness, far from home,
Vultures fret around my cries,
Now I mourn: "I am alone!"

Smells, they find me—oh so sweet,
Hunger travels to my head,
Takes me now to thy warm treat,
Luscious drink of blooming red!

Underneath a veil of flesh,
Pulsing, pumping, from the bed,
I now drink, my purpose fresh,
I now drink 'til you are dead.

Shadow and Fire

She emerged from dark, from loss, from grief,
Nurtured was the soul of disbelief,
In seclusion, brewing hate is chief,
From the dark, she scales her massif.

'Neath the moon all folk are full of cries,
From a shadow where foul death applies,
Cutting victims under the black skies,
Is the creature of no compromise.

Terror surges out in vein-like streams,
Soaring now, she tries to aid their screams,
Tangled in the Shadow's dreadful dreams,
Beaten down and agony now teems.

Prisoned deep within a woeful vale,
Hanging, crucified by rusted nail,
Ripping free and burning down her jail,
Tortured soul now cracks her vengeful tail.

Blackness grows and runs the rivers red,
Shattered people sink with fears of dread,
Cowering until their hopes are dead,
Shadow grins, its misery is spread.

Thunder rumbles 'neath as clouds make room,
Shadow hunts with anger in full fume,
Rain of fire as she returns in bloom!
From the brink she seeks the monster's doom.

Clashing hard as shadow now meets light,
Hopeful people stand and watch the fight,
Furious, she toils to break the blight,
Killing darkness with her fiery might.

Brighter skies as inky waters clear,
Folk now gather round her; free of fear,
She now dies; they fall and shed a tear,
Years to come, they'll praise her deed with cheer.

Destiny

When you lay in shadows,
Fretting in your bed,
Don't you shed a tear for me;
I choose to fight the dead.

When you run through tunnels,
Hiding in the gloom,
Fear not when I don't follow,
The dark is my playroom.

I cried and hid when I was young,
So many years ago,
Zombies ate my parents' whole,
I watched them die so slow.

Raised in hidden valleys deep,
Within the mud and cold,
Forging clothes from beasts I'd slain,
Eyes wild until I'm old.

Earth is lost in ruin now,
Stolen by the dead,
They rose from graves and marched the towns,
To paint our streets blood red.

I'm clad in armored leathers,
With gauntlets strong and true,
My spear and sword and firearm,
I'm here! So rest anew.

Call me and you'll find me there,
Scream! And I'll come your way,
To fling you right behind me,
To have you live this day.

So when you're safe and sound at home,
Nestled in your bed,
Never waste your tears for me;
I *choose* to fight the dead.

Ghost

I remember the fire
as the flames crept higher,
Wooden beams blistered red,
I rushed from out my room,
fearing my final doom,
            Hall burning up ahead.

The black and swirling smoke
had forced me then to choke,
I cupped my hands and cried,
Stretching flames they towered,
on my knees I cowered,
            It was the night I died.

The pelting violent rains,
They couldn't kill the flames,
            That turned me into ash,
The brittle bones of home,
Lay burning as I roam,
            Beneath a lightning's flash.

In the dense winter's mist,
I swirl and still exist,
With loss I now linger,
My story is retold
over the years gone cold,
        It's life I now hunger.

Soul In Chains

O hear me creature, surging greatest fire!
    Be set upon my wandering, lonely soul.
O gift me Lord, the love that I desire,
    And clasp my mortal flesh and take me whole!

Near cauldrons deep where daemons lie in wake.
    I bleed within a dark and muddy grave;
With roaches burrowing, my flesh they take,
    To life's own gate, I ride a painful wave.

I scream! Emerged from out the cold wet earth!
    My soul now sold, my shell, it drips with gore.
O Lord of darkness, you have given birth—
    My love awaits on nearby, windy shore.

O sweet and gentle maiden, true embrace,
    Is prisoner now to all my offering,
Your eyes are blind to my distorted face,
    Your soul in chains, there'll be no wandering.

In valleys far from searching eyes; we live,
    Embracing now, our frozen hearts will shine.
Your duty states, devotion you will give,
    From ash to ash and dust to dust, you're mine.

The Land of the Stolen Children

The pale ones drank their forbidden rum,
As they scurried over lands of stone,
When dark clouds formed to shield the sun,
Their sights would pierce through skin and bone.

My daughter laid upon a bed of straw,
Wrapped in a rug sewn with red,
I guarded the window 'til my eyes grew sore,
In those misty lands of the dead.

This is a tale that would pain your heart,
Inked on parchments torn and true,
When darkness comes, the nightmare will start,
With fangs so vast, they'll run you through.

Plucked from their beds, one by one,
Children were stolen into the night,
To be turned into those that fear the sun,
Their eyes veined red, their skin so white.

I tired from being a slave,
To the ghastly terrors that dwell around,
I cradled my girl that I longed to save,
Kissing her forehead and setting her down.

With a necklace of garlic and wooden cross,
I dared to pass the village gate,
Stepping over rocks of wilted moss,
I ventured out to test my fate.

With a loaded musket, I pushed my search,
Through the tunnels of the forest, diving deep,
In the dark hollows within trees of birch,
The burrow appeared where the pale ones' sleep.

I scattered my trap in that dark, dead place,
Tossing gun powder here and there,
In the tree tops I hid, with frost on my face,
I prayed and longed for fate to be fare.

Time slipped by, was it minutes or hours?
Creatures emerged out from the dark,
My musket, it fired, forming smoky towers,
I rejoiced as my bullet found its mark.

Their howls screeched within the fire's embrace,
I ran through the woods from the burning wake,
My heart, it pounded at a violent pace,
As the heat followed me like a monstrous snake.

I woke the town crying, 'Hell has come near!'
As the forest's glow raised higher and higher,
Everyone filled a pail and formed a frontier,
To fight in the hope the flames would retire.

Come morning Hell's mouth did not lick our gate,
As we'd drenched our borders from east to west,
The heat and smoke retreated before late,
And our stolen children were finally put to rest.

The Fifty Mile House

Cody's eyes snapped open in their dry sockets. The ringing in his ears made his head swim as he tried to gauge where the hell he was. His teeth bit into a restraint—coarse belts strapped around his skull, gagging him with a solid resin ball. The tightness had the hug of a helmet, as he could move his head freely. He shook furiously to release its grip, but whatever the apparatus was, it held fast. Strings of thick drool slimed over the wedged ball, paining his jaw, and he sucked desperate gasps of air. He was laying on his side. When he looked down at his abdomen, he expected to see his battle armour coated in blood, but what he saw made his heart freeze.

His armour was gone, replaced with a loose-fitting orange one-piece—zipped from his crotch to his neck. Sweat dripped from every pore within the chafing material. When he moved his shoulders, his heart hammered to realise that his hands were bound behind his back and his ankles were shackled. His vision toggled back and forth from double to normal; his stomach churned, vomit threatening to erupt from out of his mouth. Two blazing lights smothered him. Slamming his eyes shut, he worked himself to his knees, his back to the glare.

Where am I? Laborious breaths continued to spray drool over the ball. Mechanical levers and rods worked in the surrounds, whining and ticking, hydraulics compressing oil and working their way to his position. Tightness pressed around his arms. Two large brackets secured his body into place as though in the grasp of a giant hand. A swivel and spin worked above him. Gliding down in a steady hum, chrome-plated arms and rubber-tipped clamps reached. His head was forced down, chin to chest. Cody shook helplessly, urinating hot streams down his thighs—he finally realized where he could be.

Pressure was released from his skull and he watched the straps that braced his head drop and dangle. He coughed and worked his tongue, almost instinctively knowing that perhaps he was free of the choking hazard. The large ball, with its straps, fell to the floor with a loud thud. The robotics continued to whine and hum above his head. Cody screamed—with a strength he didn't know he had—as razor-like sensations began to etch into the back of his neck. Drops of warm blood streamed down. The agony stopped almost as soon as it'd begun and the mechanics that held him, retracted back into their places.

Restraints slackened. He freed his wrists, kicked away the shackles, and dropped.

A deafening computerized voice spoke:

Inmate: 75762057

Name: Cody Hodges.

Weight: 79 Kilograms.

Age: 39 years.

Occupation: Former Soldier, Red Core Regiment.

Rank: Infantry.

Violation: Desertion.

Sentence: Indefinite.

Cody burst out a raging cough, overwhelmed to the reality of where he was. *I'm fifty miles out from Melbourne. Can't be the city lock-up, that doesn't have unmanned, examination chambers like this…*

The irony, he thought, coughing out again, *robotics in a human prison…*

The original human community agreed with the use of technology, but the Technological Society (TS), not only used it, but had robotics as part of their anatomy.

Cody tried to shake thoughts from his throbbing head—static news footage of explosions, riots, and burning cars. In the dawn of 2019, the conflict between the TS and the original human community had begun – 'The Great Human Divide.' He could see the adverts, flashing before him as he gasped for air. Blond women with perfect faces, showcasing the introduction of the Enhanced Brain Chip (EBC), a glowing blue light blinking above their left ears. Title cards flashed, 'Record and scroll through your day! Need to study up about an important meeting? Just read it, store it away, and recall it when the time is right! You'll never have to remember a thing!'

Cody shut his eyes, memories of when the governments were overcome with EBC members. In 2025, unrest hit the streets; the EBC was made mandatory. Billboards flashed, 'Be compatible with the ever-growing world!' Watching the news, he remembered dropping his beer over the kitchen floor, scrolling headlines stating, 'TS military make their move into major cities, globally! The Human Resistance has started revolt! Governments predict war in 2027!'

Vibrations rumbled the shiny white floor beneath him, and he was snapped into the present. The floor gave way. Hurling a stream of yellow bile, his body spiralled down the sharp turns of the black slide from hell. The ride was rough, grooved and etched with dints that chafed every part of his body. A bright light loomed ahead as he screamed, tumbled and slid across a gravel surface.

Coughing out a mouthful of dust, blinking his dry eyes clear, nothing but yellows, oranges and browns filled his sight. He was outdoors; as much as you *could* be in the year 2057. His joints screamed with every attempt to stand. He was weak, and the world swam around him. The glare of the red, clouded sky was tinted by a circular, glass oxygen dome. Voices echoed, and numerous pairs of feet shuffled in the dust meters away. His pounding ears picked up odd mutterings here and there.

"Fresh meat, hey, Kane?"

"He's mine first, Koch!"

Cody forced out another dry cough that burned his throat. Stumbling to his feet, he scanned the exercise yard. Dozens of eyes were on him. Muttering voices called to him.

"How are ya, sweetheart?"

"Yeah, you look like a nice unit, eh? I'll loosen you up."

The muttering grew into laughter, cheers and whistles. Ignoring the taunts, he stumbled towards one of the four walls of the yard. With a mouth starving for water, he snapped his gaze to a clatter of voices to his right. A grey wall, lined with exposed latrines, had an audience. Tottering backward, he looked over the shoulders of two inmates sitting nervously on the toilets. Scanning over the onlookers, the pulse of heavy breathing assaulted his ears. His tired eyes saw the tugging of penises. Gasping voices were uttering in fits of pleasure that made his gut churn.

"Oh, yeah… fuckers…"

"Hey, that's what I'm talkin' about!"

"Come on, don't be princesses. Spread your legs? Give us a show?"

Stepping away from the inmates sickening peepshow, he found himself being hauled to the nearest wall. Before he knew it, his right cheek was planted on the grey concrete surface. The weight of a broad hand pressed upon his skull, keeping him in place. The rub of an erect penis forced him to dry retch as it dragged up and down his behind, along with the weight of a heavy body that reeked of year-old sweat. Struggling was hopeless; he was too weak. A slimy, warm tongue licked up the side of his face; chuckles from nearby echoed in his ears. A cold sweat covered him afresh as he panted.

"You taste good, bitch," said a deep voice into his ear.

Every muscle cramped to a deafening buzzer, which sounded from somewhere high above. A siren. Going on and off, on and off.

"Looking forward to seeing you next time, fucker…" the voice said again. A hard fist was driven into the side of his gut and he dropped to the dirt. Blurred vision revealed heavy feet walking away, along with the rest of the herd.

Rolling onto his back, rubbing his eyes, he stared up at the dome, coughing as the siren continued to blare. The walls at either side stretched up to impossible heights. The tips of four watchtowers stretched higher still, each graced with a missile launcher. Lying, exhausted, coughing and staring, he repeated through his cracked lips, "I'm in fucking jail… I'm in fucking jail… I'm in…"

Cody had lost consciousness at some point, perhaps when he was alone in the dirt; he couldn't be sure. What was certain was the grey square room around him. Looking about in the silence and taking in some deep breaths, he raised himself up from the bed, which was nothing more than a rubber-coated slab that protruded from the wall.

No pillow.

No blanket.

Air temperature looked to be controlled, but that was it.

Looking down at himself, his heart skipped. A hot flush washed over his face. *My photo!* He patted the side of his arm; in his combat gear, a pocket rested there, and within that pocket was his faded photo of Carrie.

No…

Cody rubbed at his face as a lump developed in his throat. He thought about his family, memories stabbing his mind to the point where he couldn't decipher what was thought or reality. He reached out his hand, thinking he could touch Carrie and Ava's faces, their tears, as he left for the zone. Ava had been a newborn and had cried amongst their misery. The image of their despair tore him apart inside. He wanted to get back to them more than anything, but contact was denied for Prime Operatives like himself, to keep them focussed and free from distraction.

There were two main divisions within the Resistance. The Prime Operations consisted of highly-trained soldiers, specialising in all forms of combat as well as being educated in cyber warfare. The enlisted branch of the Resistance was the Red Core. Accountants, teachers, postmen, farmers… trained to fire a weapon and get to the end of an obstacle course without throwing up.

He recalled the computerised voice stating that he was registered from the Red Core; his Prime rank had been stripped. The war machine in him stirred in his chest, but the human being that wanted nothing more but to lay his eyes upon his family couldn't care less.

He ran tender fingers over the back of his neck.

The prison etchings were still fresh and stung to the touch. Despite his quickening heart and his sudden sorrow, he was at the very least, himself again. He leaned against one of the walls, his mind struggling for the last thing he could remember before being awoken by blinding lights.

What happened to the transporter craft? He rubbed the top of his head. *It wasn't an enemy raid or a land mine. If it were either, I'd be in pieces. What the fuck happened? Whatever it was, they found me and knew I'd run.*

Shit.

A deafening buzzer snapped him again to the present and a door rolled up in the wall before him. The computerised voice repeated:

Proceed in an orderly fashion to the exercise yard. Disruptive inmates will receive no food privileges for 24 hours…

Stepping out into the procession of marching inmates, back straight and hands at his sides, he followed suit. Flesh goosed on his arms when he looked at some of the others; their eyes were vacant. A tingle of razors worked at the marks on his neck and all of a sudden, he felt as though he had no control over his body. He was an observer to his own movements, which had taken him out into the light of the exercise yard. The back of his neck pained him again and he stumbled a few steps, as though released from a moving platform. A chill washed over his flesh and he opened and closed his hands, restoring circulation.

The other prisoners went about their herding, going into groups, chatting and shoving. Some laughed, and others just leaned against the great walls and looked up at the red sky.

Orange clouds lingered.

A distant rumble shook the ground.

Cody braced and looked up. The inmates didn't seem to care. He knew it was the distant conflict, perhaps the war of Perth; the TS had been trying to take Perth for nearly a month. Looking up at the rocket launchers perched on the south-facing tower, he squinted to see that the smaller machine guns were facing into the yard, tracking movements—keeping the inmates in check. Before Cody could even think about finding a place to remain unnoticed, he found himself shoved into a corner. His back slammed hard against the grey concrete as four inmates closed in.

The largest one of them said, "You're my new bitch."

"I don't snuggle, thanks," Cody said, stretching his neck, all weakness gone.

"Looks like he doesn't get it, Kane," said the shortest of the four.

"Traitors normally don't," Kane said with a shrug. He was

a tank of man, overweight, and towered them all by a foot.

Cody straightened and fisted his hands.

"That's right, isn't it, bitch? Word is you're a deserter. A worthless run-away."

"I'm not running now."

Kane laughed. "I'm gonna make your arse bleed, whore!"

"I told you before: I don't snuggle."

"But you'll squeal like a pig," he said with a grin.

Kane launched one of his broad fists at Cody's face, but it met the hard wall. Cody dropped and threw two fast, hard punches into the groin. Kane hit the dirt clutching his testicles. Cody hopped from his knees, skilfully dodging the three other attacks. Weaving left and right to punches he saw a mile away, he landed elbows into chins, flat hands into throats, and a swinging heal into the back of a head. He stood over the four inmates who nursed their broken noses, swelling balls, or light concussions in the settling dust.

"Learn from this," Cody said, barely breaking a sweat. "Corner me again and I'll take your fucking heads off."

Walking away, a burning tingle tracked the marks on the back of his neck. A surging pain followed. Kane and his followers also clutched at their markings. The computerised voice said:

Inmates 75762057, 85252055, 77442056, 35462025 and 00242032. You are in violation of the conduct code and are removed from food privileges for 24 hours. Confinement necessary.

Twenty-four hours in a plain cell of concrete felt like a week. Sleep was hopeless. Cody couldn't find a position remotely resembling comfort on the rubber-coated slab, and he must have sat in every inch of floor space to stop himself from thinking. However, he couldn't escape himself…

…The stale taste of the air from his oxygen tank, lingered on his tongue like old cheese. The wind whistled, and clouds birthed at his feet as he stood in position in the sandy trench. Through his red-eye lenses, he watched his captain pace down the line of Prime Operatives. Before every mission, it was Captain Burnett's custom to give every man a personal briefing, to ensure each operative knew exactly what they had to do. Although the mission was the priority, Burnett never looked at his men as drones or expendable pawns to help advance a position. Burnett cared for his operatives and their roles within any assault. The aim was to complete every task with the least amount of unit casualties. This strategy made Captain Burnett's unit an efficient one.

They were sixty yards away from a TS outpost. The mainframe housed within it was a direct link to the TS Corp's network. These armoured bunkers were stationed around the zone to allow optimum communications with TS forces on the ground and in the air. The mission was to take the position and steal intelligence. However, it was surrounded by T-Assault Units, but the Resistance called them 'X-Heads.' They were robotic drones with heavily-plated torsos, machine guns mounted at the hips and upon their arms, and long grasshopper-like legs carried them. The steel-plated heads, with two beady red-eye lenses and thick cabling snaking out of the ear positions to the side of the neck, were nestled between thick shoulder frames. These machines were manufactured not just for warfare, but to inflict as much suffering to the human body as possible. Suicide was better than being captured by one.

Ten of them guarded the bunker.

Cody straightened and saluted as Burnett was in front of him.

"At ease, Hodges," said Burnett through his mask, his eyes barely visible from the round-eye lenses. His voice was muffled through the oxygen filter. Over the next few moments, Burnett proceeded to outline the plan for the bunker assault. Cody struggled to focus, continually shaking images of his family's faces from his head—he always feared that every mission carried a one-way ticket.

"Got that, Hodges?"

"Yes, Captain."

Burnett gave him a nod and left for the next operative. Cody received enough to know he was with the unit going through the centre. Adjusting his helmet, he cleaned the sights of his assault blaster, and checked the pulse resistor fixed to his waist belt; this unit sent pulses of electronic barbs down into the sand every few seconds, repelling the dangers that lurked underfoot. Rising from the ashes of the nuclear aftermath back in 2023, changing and adapting, nature had created a new enemy while mankind was fighting amongst itself. The barbs kept them at bay.

Cody readied his stance against the sandy trench and moderated his breathing, trying to relax as much as possible until it was time. He glided a hand over the pocket to his arm; a faded photo of Carrie rested there; she was thirty weeks pregnant. Before long, Burnett passed him and positioned himself a few operatives down. Cody tightened his grip on his weapon, awaiting the signal. A small beeping note sounded in the comm of his right ear, and the east and west teams lined the red sky with the white pathways of their grenades.

Cody lost his footing as the impact of the bombing shower rocked the dunes and a second signal spiralled through his ear canal. He was over the top and into the dust clouds. A scatter of blue bullet fire came from the clouds ahead—the X-Heads were firing in random directions at the unit's unseen approach. Cody dropped to the sand. He aimed, thumbing a button, focussing his weapon's sights. Silhouettes of the crude, skeletal droids were sighted through the targeting scope. Cody caught one in the crosshair and fired—he was a good shot.

The X-Head rocked about on its destroyed legs and fell back when further fire to its arms hit home. Heavy rounds continued from the rest of the centre unit, all following the same strategy. Everything had gone according to plan, and they advanced. Within a few moments, all the X-Heads were in pieces.

The operatives gathered at the door of the bunker within the waves of amber dust caught in the winds. Burnett stood before Cody and another operative and said, "Hodges, Banks: Nuke the entrance! This isn't over. There are more inside!"

They set their charges. Everyone scattered for cover. The door blasted outward. Cody and Banks led the charge to either side of the destroyed doorway. An alarm sounded from inside, lights flashed within the mix of smoke and fire extinguisher gas.

Burnett halted, checking the scanning device on his forearm. "Wait!" he said holding up his left fist—all operatives behind him halted, their firearms at the ready. "Something has changed," he said, "I'm registering multiple—"

Cody saw what happened next as though it was in slow motion. The X-Head at Burnett's feet, gripped its robotic hand around his ankle and detonated. Its eruption was a short-range blast, enough to shred through the Captain's legs like a meat grinder. The side of his mask was caught in the shrapnel, ripping apart in a spray of steel, flesh and bone. Burnett's body dropped as every other X-Head—seemingly neutralized—detonated in a succession of blasts that shook the earth. Cody's ears rang as limbs, body armour, weapons and torsos flew about in the air. He snapped his gaze to Banks, who was frozen at the sight of their entire unit being blown apart.

"Banks! Status!" Cody yelled through his comm. "Banks! Wake the fuck up! Are you injured?"

Banks turned to him and screamed through his mask, "What the hell do we do now?"

"What we came to do!"

Cody entered the bunker and descended the stairs with Banks in tow. The smoke was clearing, and the grill of the corridor floor was in sight. Two TS-Corp soldiers fired up at them. The TS infantry were fast shooters, and light on their feet due to their thin, black uniforms and gloss-coated battle masks. However, their armour was easy to penetrate, especially when the Resistance's standard bullet gauge had enough force to penetrate two-inch steel. Cody and Banks both set their blasters to automatic fire and lit up the corridor. They advanced past the devastated bodies—Banks firing an extra few rounds into the corpses for good measure—and they went to work.

With a memorised routine, they clicked and snapped their blasters together to form a small rocket launcher. They hit the control room door and took cover when it exploded with a blast of melted steel. They each rolled in a smoke grenade and engaged three more of the TS, shooting holes through their heads and chests. One of the TS-Computer operatives was left in his control chair with his hands up. He was an overly-skinny man with a long skeletal face, sunken eyes, short grey hair, and his EBC flickering a blue light above his left ear—processing and receiving data. He was trembling where he sat.

Both Cody and Banks had their aim on him, inching closer. "Up off the chair and step away from the console," Cody said.

"You originals are fighting a lost war. You will never defeat us," he said in a voice that tingled with electricity—as though the voice was coming from an external source, and he was just the transmitter—the sight ran a chill up Cody's spine.

"I didn't ask for your fucking opinion. Out of the chair and away from the console!"

"The TS will succeed in taking your barrier city of Melbourne. New York. Berlin. Paris. Sydney… You're finest strongholds. Gone. Nothing you do here will achieve anything. Surrender yourselves to—"

The technician's head exploded as a round of Banks's blaster sent echoes through the bunker. Blood, brain matter, microchips, wires and bone scattered the control boards, and the body slouched to the side. Banks stepped up to the decapitated body, gripped it by the left shoulder and discarded it like a rag doll. Swivelling the bloodied chair on its wheels, he positioned it before the largest of the five screens. Slinging his weapon over his shoulder, stripping off his gloves, he went to work on the keyboard, skilfully inputting a series of hacking formulas.

Cody kept guard, looking over his shoulder every few seconds. "How long?"

"It'll take me a few minutes to override their security codes. I'm in a countdown. If I don't break the firewall, this bunker is gonna blow."

"I'll shut up then."

"Appreciate it."

Sweat dripped down Cody's back. He was trembling and taking in deep, hoarse breaths through his air mask. A beeping sounded from the console and the alarms about the bunker had turned off. "I'm in!"

"The network? You achieved access?"

"Commencing upload of all tactical data. I've found their X-Head manufacturing sheets. Fuck! It has everything! Technical readouts. Structural drawings. Even on the robotics used to build them! I've accessed our server, everything is uploading now…"

"We've done it?"

They both flinched as a loud alarm thundered from the

bunker and red lights flashed from the ceiling. "What the fuck?" Cody said.

Banks turned to the screens to diagnose what had been tripped. "Detonation," he said, sighing.

"The bunker is gonna blow anyway?"

"Yeah, in thirty seconds."

"Let's get the fu—"

"—I can't! I need to monitor the upload; ensure the TS don't try and hack it. It won't be long," he said tapping at the red progress bar on the black screen. "I have to stay until it's finished and deactivate the link to our server. Priority one. You go, Cody."

"I can't leave you, Banks!"

"You've got a family, you fuck! Get out of here! I'll run out if I can!" Banks said giving him a strong punch to the shoulder.

Cody backed away and they saluted, then he ran as hard as he could. Outside, he climbed the dune trench and leaped over. Rolling down in a cloud of dust, the bunker erupted. The mushroom cloud rose into the red sky. Darting his head from side to side, his heart skipped as he lay upon the sand. He checked his barb unit and was relieved to see that it was still active. He had to stay awake. Had to move.

When he tried to stand, all went black.

The world was moving. Rumbles beneath his back flicked his dry lids to open; he was in a transport. Raising his heavy head, what he'd hope to see were medics, but what he saw were a huddle of Red Core Regiment soldiers. He looked down at himself—he was still armoured, the sand and blood spatters from his last mission still evident on his chest and arm plates. "Hey, sleeping beauty is up," said a voice near him.

"About time, we're nearly at the chopper."

"Where am I?" Cody said, as his teeth crunched on dust and sand particles that lined the walls of his mouth.

"Operative Cody Hodges? Welcome to Red Core Twelve. I'm Captain Briggs. You've been moved to assist us in our mission out south. We're about to hit a TS bunker, a few miles from where you were found. We're boarding a chopper and will be dropped into position. We're gonna hit the bunker from above and hit it hard."

"Wait a minute. Where's Banks? Where's—"

"—None from your Prime Core Unit survived, son, but you achieved your objective, as far as I know. Your intelligence would be handy for our attack."

Cody sat up, his head swimming. His vision moved in and out of focus. A gurgle churned his stomach and his ears rang. *Another mission? No. That wasn't the deal. I should be on a week's leave. There's been a mistake!*

He knew the mission was a one-way ticket; Carrie and Ava's faces flashed in his mind. He'd been in the war zone for over two years… As he sat up, the transport ground to a stop and the soldiers began to depart.

"Move it, Hodges. On your feet. You can detail me when we're in the air!" Captain Briggs said over the thunder of the awaiting chopper.

Cody slipped out of the transporter truck, watching the infantry run into a wall of swirling dust. Another transport was approaching: a cargo haul. It was heading home. Without thinking, he leapt onto the tailgate and didn't look back…

A familiar buzzer snapped Cody back to the present, and he stood from his place as the computerized voice said:

All inmates proceed to the corridor. Food privileges have been postponed.

In the exercise yard, his stomach rumbled; he couldn't remember the last time he ate. Cody stepped quickly to a spare spot on the north-facing wall. He scanned the orange-suited community as they went about their groupings. Some rubbed at the backs of their necks, cursing at the burning sensations they felt there. Cody pin-pointed Kane's position with those of his three bruised followers. They were silent, but Kane glared at him through the clutter of the other inmates.

"You're in for it, soldier," said a voice at his side. "You hurt Kane, now he wants to hurt you. Badly. Impressive moves by the way."

Cody turned his gaze to a short and stocky inmate who held out a hand for him to shake. "I'm Ades. Don't worry, I don't like Kane either."

"He picked the fight," Cody said with a shrug. "I just finished it." He didn't return the gesture.

"You leavin' me hangin'?"

"Don't take it personally. How am I to know that Kane hadn't sent you over here?"

Ades shrugged and dropped his hand. "You're vigilant, I can respect that. Not trusting anyone in here is a smart move. I should know, I've been here since 2037."

"What did you do? Wear a kid's head like a hat?" said

Cody as he scanned the prison yard through narrowed eyes.

"What? I'm no psycho. I was just dumb, drugged and paranoid. Thought these young punks were trying to steal from my auto shop, so I wacked the lot of them. Turns out I was wrong. All they were lookin' for was shelter; it was stormy that night." He raised his chin to Cody. "I hear you ran out on your squad?"

"How does that shit spread? I thought this place was air-tight!"

"The guards hate you more than anyone out here. They leak info if they want a crim to suffer."

"So inmates don't care to lose a day's worth of food?"

"Not much to miss. We just get fed protein pellets that make you shit bricks."

A distant rumble shook underfoot. Some inmates looked jittery but most shrugged it off. Cody continued his scan of the yard and locked sights on the observation window some yards away. Behind the glass, guards paced hastily down the corridor. They weren't in their standard blue uniforms. They were wearing black battle gear. Cody looked up at the tower missile launchers and his heart hammered.

Another distant rumble.

"You look spooked," said Ades.

"Look up," said Cody, turning to him.

"What?"

"Look up, tell me what you see."

Ades gave the dome a glance with a small tilt of his head and a raised eyebrow. "The dome. Radiation clouds. The towers.

"What's on top of the towers?"

"Missile launchers," Ades said with a shrug.

"All the weaponry was pointing south yesterday, with the machine guns pointing in here. Nothing is aiming at us anymore. All the artillery is facing out," Cody said. He stormed off towards the observation window.

"What the hell does that mean?"

"Hell's coming."

"Hey, wait! Where are you going? Are you nuts? They'll send a bolt of electrodes to that barcode in your skin!"

"I'll take my chances."

"You might want to keep your eye on Kane. He's moving too. I'm not getting involved."

"I didn't ask."

Cody got within two meters of the glass. Inmates looked at him as though he was a lunatic. He halted and peered inside. Unnoticed, he scanned the goings on, observing the guard seated before a terminal. Cody couldn't see the screen but strained his eyes to decipher a sequence of flashing patterns reflecting back from the terminal, over the contours of the guard's chest plate; the colour codes sent a trail of spikes up his back.

Three quick reds—two slow blues—five flickering greens. A Distress call.

The guard at the terminal noticed him. He stood and rapped the glass, saying in a muffled voice, "Move the fuck on, inmate!"

Cody took a step back and saw another guard snapping his gaze towards him. He was armoured in heavier gear than the others and drew a close resemblance to an operative from Prime Core, aside from walking with a limp. With his orange round-eye lenses boring right into Cody's face, he stepped closer to the glass. The mask tilted, suggesting: *What the hell?*

My lucky day, Cody thought to himself. *The Warden.*

Cody straightened, slammed his feet together and saluted. The Warden tilted his helmet again, bemused. Movement in the reflection of the window caught the corner of Cody's eye, and he ducked fast enough to miss a swinging arm from Kane. He caught Kane with a heavy left upper-cut to the jaw, ducked and rose with a right forearm into Kane's broad face, sending him into the glass. The pane wobbled with the impact. Cody looked back at Kane's followers, who'd kept their distance this time.

Kane staggered, rubbing at his bleeding nose; he lunged again. Cody relaxed, dodged the attack, landed a knee to the gut and a right elbow to the back of the neck, planting Kane face down in the dust. Turning back to the glass, he stepped towards it. More guards had stopped either side of the Warden, some turning their helmets hesitantly from their leader to the glass, not sure on what to do.

Cody was an inch away and mouthed: "I can help."

The Warden stood back and stabbed a finger to the side hatch—the chamber that leads in and out of the exercise yard. Sealed inside, a letterbox-like slot opened on the door leading into the observation corridor. The Warden's lenses were staring in at him. "Inmate *75762057*, you've got my attention. What do you want?"

"My name is Cody Hodges, sir, I—"

"—you're a deserter. You don't have the right to a name

anymore. You've got sixty seconds."

"I've noticed the prison has gone into lockdown. You're sending out distress signals. I know we're about to be attacked."

"You're pretty observant considering you're Red Core."

"I'm a Prime Operative, sir."

"That's not what I have on file."

"Then your files are wrong. I served under Captain Burnett."

"If that's true, it makes your desertion all the worse!"

"I didn't desert Captain Burnett. We completed our mission. Operative Banks and I were the last ones left and we *did* infiltrate that bunker. We uploaded intelligence to our server!"

A distorted sigh came from the Warden. "You were found in cargo transport that wasn't scheduled to leave base. Other deserters were on board. Security protocol activated, and the craft was gassed. The Prime mask saved you; designed to filter out toxins. There you were: fast asleep... You were supposed to be on mission with Captain Briggs."

"What happened to—"

"—They were hit in the air. You should've died with those men."

"The Resistance shouldn't have sent Red Core to do a Prime's directive! It was a waste!"

"I don't always agree with the orders handed down by the generals, I grant you that. I just got told that I wouldn't be receiving reinforcements for at least ten hours."

"How far away is the enemy?"

"Five hours."

"What have you planned?"

"Why should I be sharing my strategies with a coward?"

"Judge me all you want. It doesn't change anything about the hell that's on our doorstep. I did what I did because I wanted to go home. I was being sent on a suicide mission as thanks for my two years in the zone. I was told I was being sent home for a week, but I guess that was bullshit so I could follow orders." He stared at the warden. "I'm no coward. I'm just a pissed-off operative that made a bad judgment call. You know I can help you."

Silence.

The warden sighed. "My name is Cole Harding," he said. "I led a unit in Prime Core a while back before the dune wars started. I was appointed here seven years ago after I lost my foot in action; hence my limp. We're gonna get hit pretty hard, Hodges."

Cody raised himself to his feet and steadied his breathing. "Why doesn't the TS just light this place up? Why are they going to try and take it? The position is out of range to have any military advantage."

"The missile launchers, Hodges. They want the technology. Remember, some of the scientists in the Resistance were part of the teams responsible for designing and engineering the Brain Enhancement Chip that started this whole human fucking divide. They've designed some pretty neat weaponry for our war efforts, these launchers included. They have smarts other TS wizards don't. So, the TS want the launchers and they want to use it in their campaign to take down the Melbourne defences."

"So you've been ordered to defend the prison rather than evacuate?"

"No one can leave until reinforcements arrive and the position is held. I have no power to alter your sentence, Hodges. All I can say is that your priority is to try and live through this. It's your only hope to get back home."

"What are you planning with the defences?"

"I only have a team of thirty scared guards. They're not soldiers. We've got the outer gates sealed. We'll be stationed on the upper levels, using the defence bunkers that were designed for such an occasion. We could use an experienced gun."

"What about the inmates?" Cody said gesturing his head to the yard's entrance.

"They'll just have to wait it out."

"There's over forty prisoners out here. That's *forty* extra guns."

"Where will they be aiming, Hodges? You expect me to hand over weapons to a bunch of murderers and rapists?"

"They're in this as much as we are. They're human; original, like us. No enhancements other than the fucking compliance codes etched into their necks! Maybe *some* will fight with us."

Harding fell silent. Cody paced in the chamber, rubbing the back of this neck and looking at the letterbox opening every few seconds.

"How about this. If you feel so strongly about being a humanitarian with that scum, then *you* lead them. They'll be your unit. I'll send a compliance pulse out in the yard to ensure they'll hear you out. When the pulse is stopped, then they can make up their own minds. Whoever you get will come back here into the chamber. I'll brief you after that."

"Yes, sir." Cody saluted before turning to the exit door.

He looked over his shoulder when Harding said, "One thing, Hodges. Where I'm gonna send you, you're gonna wish you'd left them in the yard."

Cody signalled Harding through the glass. The door slid open and he stepped through, all the volunteers in tow, Ades included. Out of the forty-three inmates, a team of twenty-five agreed to put their lives on the line. The remaining, including Kane and his followers, told Cody to go fuck himself. He couldn't help but feel a little relieved; he had enough to worry about. Once in the chamber, the deafening buzzer sounded, and the computerized voice said:

Volunteers: Form a line in the corridor, inmate 75762057 remain in the chamber for briefing.

Cody gave Ades a nod as the group passed. Once alone, Harding spoke through the opening.

"Well, I wasn't expecting so many."

"I wasn't expecting so few," Cody said.

Harding nodded. "This prison was designed to be fortified in case of an attack like this. You'll be stationed in an outer trench. There is a sealed access chamber leading towards it. The gear for your men will be waiting there."

"Hang on," Cody said, frowning. "You're putting us outside?"

"I told you it wasn't going to be pretty."

"I take it there are electrical barbs around the perimeter of the trench? You know, to keep back the—"

"—We'll have them active for as long as possible. But when the TS are within range, we'll need to direct as much power as we can to the launchers. This place is already running dry. We have just enough to power two of them."

"If those barbs are turned off, sir, we're all dead!"

"It's the best I can do. That trench was specially designed for combat use. Take charge of those men, and we might be able to hold off the TS until reinforcements arrive. If we fail, then it's onto plan B."

"You're going blow the prison?"

A curt nod. "That's right. The TS will get nothing out of this," Harding said, then his helmet looked down as though he was accessing a control panel. A few beeps followed, and a small hatch opened by the observation door; within lay a standard-issue attack uniform and armour. "That's for you. It's the last set of gear we have."

"What's going to the inmates?"

"Enough talking, Hodges. I need to get to my guards."

"Hang on!" Cody said as he gathered the gear and dropped it at his feet. "What weapons are you leaving us?"

"For the inmates, everything is down in the chamber and the trench. As for you, there's our last Prime Blaster. You're lucky we had a spare."

Cody started slipping into the leg armour. "How many are going to hit us?"

"Everything … I've got to go."

"Give me something. Are they X-Heads?" Cody said, strapping the armour over his arms and locking in his shoulder plates.

"That's what the scopes have picked up."

"Any tanks coming?"

"I told you. *Everything* is coming."

"Holy shit." Cody fixed on his helmet and activated the breather. He waited as the mouthpiece fell into position between his lips and he drew in a deep breath. Through the small status screen in his visor, he noted the air tank was half empty. "Ten hours. Why the hell aren't we getting support sooner?"

"The reinforcements are coming from Perth, not Melbourne."

"Why there?"

"Although the conflict is still going, the containment lines have held. When the Resistance can free up the air squadron, they'll fly over. Melbourne is in lock-down due to *this* attack. The Resistance is not sharing an inch of resource there, just in case we don't hold the line. Just know this, if that air support gets here, the TS won't advance. They're weaker than they make themselves out to be. Get down there and organise your group."

The letterbox opening slid closed.

Cody took a long breath as the exit doors hissed open.

After clipping on his Prime Blaster and securing it to his back, he brought Ades into the trench chamber first. The equipment was neglectfully tossed into heaps. Cody stepped about the motley crew of gear, moving the dribs and drabs about with his boot. There wasn't much, but it would be enough. Helmets, gloves, footwear and a scatter of body armour. To avoid a shit fight, he was going to have to distribute the gear himself, one inmate at a time.

Making up a complete set of gear, he passed each piece to Ades and gave instructions on assembly and fitment. When all was done, he crouched, checking the ankles of Ades' prison uniform and then assessed his wrists and neck.

"What you doing? Want to tailor me something?"

"These suits are sealed. Everyone will be protected from the radiation. I guess I don't have to ask if you've handled a weapon before?" said Cody.

"The last time I held a piece was—"

"—yeah, I know. A bad joke, sorry," Cody said looking to the door to the corridor. "I'm gonna bring them in a few at a time. I want you to assist them getting ready. You cool with that?"

"I suppose… We're gonna get wiped out, aren't we?"

"Don't talk shit. We can't go down without a—"

"—not just us. I mean, everyone. All of us originals. The TS are gonna kill every last one of us, aren't they? Look at this fucking prison. It should house thousands of scum but it only has a few dozen. What does that tell you?"

"You're wrong Ades. The TS can't kill us all. They need us."

"What the hell do you—"

"—all the circuitry in their veins? For the men, their fish don't swim, and for the women? Their eggs don't grow anymore. Get my drift? They can't kill all of us. If we lose our independence, then I'm afraid extinction would be better than their plan."

"What's that?"

"We'll be lab rats, Ades, when they're not using us for procreation. They've tried cloning, but that was a mess; made nothing but a bunch of mindless freaks."

"No shit."

The process of suiting up and checking that suits were sealed was more orderly than to be expected. Fear of the impending battle kept everyone in check. Cody pushed the lever down beside the trench door, and it grinded open, revealing the battle trench bathed in the orange wash of dusk. Heavy boots smacked the dirt, every inmate feeling the toxic heat through their suits, as though being pressed with warm irons. The trench ran along the wall of the prison for fifteen-meters. The width was four meters, and the defence wall was the height of four men. There were steel platforms bolted against the wall, in reach of the defence windows; long, rectangular, and peering out into the wasteland. The platforms were also fixed with racks to hold more artillery. Cody eyed a steel cabinet at the far side. He ran to it and slid open the doors to find the weaponry. Mounted in braces, long and black, were Remote Attack Rifles. "RARs," Cody said with a grin then turned to the men. "All right, come here and get your weapons!"

When the inmates brushed passed him to get to their pieces, he headed straight for Ades who was inspecting his weapon as though it was a toy rather than the real thing. "What the hell is this piece of—"

"—it's a Remote Attack Rifle."

"Seriously? It's too light!"

"Don't let that fool you. A round from this will melt a hole in any droid. It gets its spower from the prison grid, and is activated by a control panel up in the towers. They're all off at the moment. The Warden will activate them when we start getting some heat." Cody held out his hand to Ades. "Thanks for coming out here."

Ades accepted the gesture. "For the human race."

"Stay next to me. We'll get through this."

Movement caught Cody's sights. Spiralling over the far-right corner of the trench, surging down like a whip, was a sight that made his skin crawl.

It had been a year since he'd seen a mutant.

Like the long arm of an octopus, the tentacle—with its end of sharp bone acting like a machete—swooped down and decapitated an inmate. As the body dropped, spurting blood from between its shoulders, the tentacle swooped down again, stabbed its razor bone into another inmate's gut. The screaming prisoner was raised over the wall and out of sight. All in the trench backed away in panic, raising their dead weapons at the position of the hidden monstrosity. The gurgled screams of the inmate on the outside were soon overridden by the cracking of cartilage and the ripping of flesh. Cody turned his head when the crunching of bone bored into his eardrums; the inmate was being consumed into the beast's beak-like mouth.

"Stand back!" said Cody as he unclipped his blaster. Putting his weight to his back foot, he fired a grenade over the wall.

The detonation rocked the ground and the trench was showered in a scatter of mangled flesh, bone and twitching tentacles. He rushed up to one of the attack windows. The landscape of sand was moving. His heart hammered. Lumps of octopus-like shapes slithered about in the dune sea, all rolling and diving, heading right for them.

Cody toggled a switch at the side of his helmet. The comm crackled in his right ear, but he tried it anyway. "Harding!

Over? Turn the barbs on! The serpents are surfacing!"

A screech of feedback pierced his head as though needles were being inserted into his skull, and Harding's voice spoke some distorted words.

"We need the power! Enemy in range. RARs… on!"

"Get to a window, fire the fuck out of anything that moves!" Cody said as he set his blaster to automatic and fired fiercely.

Thunder rumbled from above.

The two launchers.

The blast force threw everyone to the ground as though they'd suffered an earthquake. Cody lifted himself up to the window. The flight paths of the two missiles cut through the red swirling clouds like a razor through cotton. The lines grew thinner and thinner into the horizon, then in the distance, a thunder rocked underfoot. The sound travelled to them, picking up dust and sand in its wake and burst every man's eardrums. Cody gripped at his helmet but maintained his sights on the horizon. Black mushroom clouds were forming on the red and orange sky.

They'd hit something. Tanks. Big fucking tanks.

Shaking his head, he continued firing out of the window. Inmates, those brave enough, took positions and fired into the desert at the horrors heading their way.

Ades was at Cody's side. "What the fuck are those things? Those monsters!" he screamed in between shots.

"Sand Serpents! Aim for the mantles!"

Another missile launch, and all were grounded.

Cody gazed out the window – two more black mushroom clouds.

The blast wave.

"Wait, what's that?" Ades said pointing at the horizon.

A constant rumble shook the platforms.

Oh fuck…

A darker line appeared in the distance, growing steadily larger. The rumble grew heavier. Inmates continued to fire upon the beasts as they closed the gap.

"X-Heads," said Cody, firing off more rounds at mantles. "They're charging."

Rapid fire erupted from the upper levels of the prison – the guards. The landscape ahead was being sprayed with a scatter of bright blue lights. Small fiery explosions lit in the distance, causing tremors underfoot as shots hit home. The trench was showered with dust as another surge from the launchers assaulted the horizon.

Black mushrooms.

Blast wave.

Screams broke from the other side of the trench, and Cody swung his gaze to where the inmates were firing at the sky.

Tentacles reached over the wall.

"Holy fuck!" yelled one of them.

The razor bone sliced off one of the inmate's legs, sending it flying and rolling, leaving a trail of dark blood on the dirt. Another long arm swirled and whooshed down, wrapping itself around a new prize and lifting it into the air.

The tentacle hauled the struggling inmate over the wall. Outside, another mantle had rolled over to join in the feasting, curling one of its tentacles around the inmate's left leg and ripping it off as though separating a chicken.

Screams were muffled as his helmet was shoved into a snapping beak.

Cody and Ades fired at the feasting giants, shredding flesh—toxic and human—until they were devastated and spread across the sand. Cody redirected fire to another rolling mantle; it exploded like a large water balloon.

More screams.

A mantle had dropped into the trench.

Tentacles whipped out and swung randomly, taking a head, half a body and a leg. Cody and Ades fired. The beast twitched and drooped in a growing pool of its own toxic grey blood. The wounded lay screaming, but Cody went back to the window. The mutants had eased their fix on the trench, starting to burrow into the sand. The brown line that was once on the horizon was like a wall in the near distance.

The death wave.

Their steel bodies were formed into wheels, treading the surface at great speed. One hundred strong, at least.

"Fire at them, fire!"

They kicked up clouds upon clouds of sand, creating a tidal wave in tow. Explosions erupted from the line as rounds from the trench hit home. Cody had a jolt to his spirits as the inmates were surprisingly good shooters. X-Head after X-Head were folding, buckling, tripping and sending others either side of them to the dirt. Pieces of robotic apparatus were flung into the air.

All kept hammering their triggers, crosshairs darting from unit to unit as they approached. A wave of impact rattled at the platforms; the X-Heads dug their legs into the sand, skidding yards upon yards until settling into a march, aiming their artillery and firing instantly.

Bullets showered the trench windows; Ades and Cody dropped for cover. An inmate was hurtled backward, his chest and the face of his mask spotted with steaming rounds. His body twitched, lying in a growing blood pool.

It was joined by another body. Then another.

Cody spun around and hauled Ades with him to the prison wall. The crunch of steel on stone cut the air; the machines were scaling the walls. There weren't many inmates left. Two had retreated into the trench's chamber; Cody didn't blame them. The remaining four had the courage to stay with their backs to the prison, firing shot after shot at the hint of robotics that protruded over the wall. Cody kicked the cover off the control panel to the trench door. Sliding out a small unit, which converted into a mini computer terminal, he frantically tapped away at the keyboard.

"What are you doing?" Ades yelled.

"Sending an override to the towers. We're dead meat if I don't try something!"

Cody tapped furiously as his heart raced to the point of bursting. Hydraulics hissed and hummed from above and he stared up. The smaller artillery redirected sights to the trench wall. He snapped a gaze back at the terminal—its black and green screen flashing an activation alert—and he hit the enter key.

The thunder from above was deafening.

A machine-gun pulse rained on the outside of the trench. Explosions erupted and soon Cody, Ades and the inmates were being showered with robotic remains. Although the towers continued to fire rapidly, sights engaging unit after unit and reducing them to scrap metal, it didn't stop them.

Before they knew it, an X-Head was over the top.

Then another.

An inmate decided to charge one of them, firing as he ran. The skeletal droid, partly damaged, didn't return fire. It engaged him, locking a metal hand to his throat and lifting him two feet off the dirt. Its free hand released a circular saw from its palm. It started up, whining into action. The X-Head jostled the struggling inmate within its chokehold and sawed off his right and left arms as though de-branching a tree with devastating ease. Before it got to his legs, Cody lit them up.

More X-Heads dropped over into the trench, some were in pieces, and others were still active enough to be deadly. Cody and Ades fought back-to-back, sending bolt-shattering rounds. Two X-heads had stumbled into the chamber, sparking cables and damaged robotics in tow. Cody's blood ran cold when the whining of their saws roared from within, then following that, the screams.

"They're sawing them up!" Ades said, his voice breaking.

"It's what they're built to do. If one gets close, it's programmed to disembowel. You could either suffer that or blow yourself away… It's your call."

Cody stepped towards the chamber of screams and launched in a grenade. The detonation sent a shower of shrapnel from out the doorway. They hit the ground. Looking about the trench, none of the other inmates were standing. Joint from joint, they were being cut apart whilst they screamed. The sight ate at Cody's marrow. He scrambled into the billowing smoke with Ades in tow.

The doors enclosed them into the smoke-filled chamber, which carried the scent of burning metal and roasting meat. They both coughed, burning their throats. X-Heads rammed the door, rapping with their metal fists. Cody fired a round into the control panel, eliminating any chance of the droids overriding the door. The thunder of the battle showered them with dust.

"We need to get to higher ground," Cody gasped. He felt his way through the thick smoke, flicked a switch at a comm unit and spoke. "Harding, do you copy? Permission to come up and assist."

"Roger," came an unrecognizable, distorted voice.

Cody looked back at the Ades as he was coughing out a lung; the red lenses of his helmet a blur through the smoke. "Get over here, we'll be out of this smoke chamber in a minute."

Ades began to stumble when the chamber door opened, and a guard was silhouetted in the doorway.

As though in slow motion, the guard fired a round at Ades' position. His lenses went out. A splatter and a thud came next, sending ice up Cody's back. Without thinking, he lunged, pulled at the arm that held the gun, and bent it over his shoulder ninety degrees the wrong way. The guard screamed. Cody spun round, clamped the guard's head under his arm, and cracked his neck. Dropping the body at his feet, he stumbled to Ades through the smoke.

Like a blind man, he reached down for him, but he knew what the status would be.

Gone.

Cody entered the corridor, the lights flickered, and dust fell from the ceiling with every vibration that came from the outdoors—the X-Heads were assaulting the prison with rocket fire. He ran to the elevator and headed for the top floor, but it stopped on the hanger level. When the door slid open, two guards were aiming into it, and upon sighting him, they immediately relaxed.

"Shit, Kreggan!" one of them said. "Hurry the fuck up! Did you get the Prime Blaster?"

Cody held it up but said nothing. He followed the guards, comfortable they didn't recognize him under the guard's attack gear. He was led to a troop carrier, which had its engines charged and firing—ready to take off. Stamping his heavy feet onto the grate of the lift as it raised him and others into the craft, they were in the air. A few seconds into the flight, the guards started talking to him.

"It was worth getting that extra blaster, hey, Kreggan? We're gonna need it when we get back to Melbourne. We may have to shoot our way in. Don't worry, I've got connections. If we get through the checkpoints, we'll have somewhere to lay low."

They laughed at the prospect and one of the others said, "What happened in that chamber, Kreggan? We couldn't see shit on the monitor because of the smoke. Bet it felt good to drop that Prime crook. The deserter, right?"

He nodded, his flesh burned at the display of hypocrisy.

Cody went to a window as the prison got smaller and smaller. Black objects dotted the red sky in the west. Like a hive, they swirled and broke into formations, getting steadily larger.

The cavalry.

Cody's lenses zoomed. Lightning bolts of heavy fire rained from the Resistance aircraft, hitting the X-Head army in the defence they'd promised. Harding was right; the squadron was death from above. Their missile fire ripped through droids as though they'd been put together with spit.

"The Warden?" Cody said in a low voice, resetting his lenses.

"Harding?" one of the guards laughed. "Have you got fucking amnesia? You're the one that put a hole in his head. It was the plan all along. We didn't sign up to die for some fucking launchers."

"No. I signed up to die for the human fucking race!"

Cody lifted his blaster and aimed through its sight. The crosshair locked on all heads as he toggled the targeting switch. Before they could do anything to react, their heads flung back in turn as rounds popped off the back of each of their skulls. The pilot fumbled with a weapon, but Cody locked an arm under his chin, snapping his head one-eighty degrees.

Rolling the body off the seat, he settled himself behind the controls. An information display typed out red words within his lenses.

Melbourne. Forty-eight miles. North.

Carrie and Ava's faces flashed into his thoughts, blast doors covering their tear-covered cheeks. *It would just take a few minutes to dock*, he thought. *I can try and be with them.* The craft rocked as the blast waves of the battle carried through the air.

U-turn.

Cody's lenses focused on the lightshow in the distance. Pulling the throttle level down, the craft rattled as the jets exploded into full speed. Cody flicked four switches above his head, charging the guns. In range, he sighted a group of X-Heads by the east wall. Calibrating locks on multiple units, he pressed the trigger.

Carrie and Ava's faces flashed again. Crying. Screaming.

I'll be home soon, he said to them. *But I need to make sure there'll be a home to go to.*

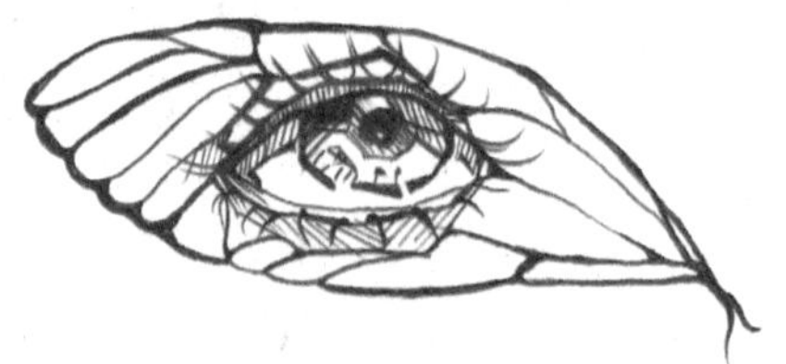

ᴀTLANTICA

1824, *Atlantic Ocean, October.*

Dearest Edna,

Please forgive the tardiness of this letter. I am writing to you whilst still out at sea, and hope to find the fortune in posting this letter back to London once we've found port in the Americas.

As I have promised, this shall be my last voyage, and through my calculations of the impending profit, I would need not undertake any further crossing through the Middle Passage of the Atlantic. Although this journey has only stretched for a week, it has already seen much misery, not only upon the poor souls that fill the slave quarters below, but even for my crew. I trust that the rewards will be worth the hardships.

I would hope, that upon my return, we can be wed. I would want for nothing more than your hand in marriage, my darling.

With you always,

Fredrick.

Captain Fredrick Phillips launched from the seat of this desk. The world weaved and rocked around him. His hair, greying and stringy, stuck to his forehead with sweat that hadn't dried in what felt like an eternity.

I must have dozed off. He took a calloused palm to his brow. Sleep was near impossible when the sea was ravaged by storms. Even with that fact, when he did find sleep, his dreams were darkened with nightmares so vicious, strangling pains would mysteriously bruise the skin around his neck. Dreams ravaged by dark, human-like shapes, monstrous and murderous. Fredrick wanted for nothing more than to be out of the sea, and for his feet to walk dry land once again.

Free from the sea.

Free from the nightmares.

Fredrick's eyes snapped back to the present. Wild and wide, they fixed on the fallen oil lamp. It was bathing his parchment with a wash of orange light. But, with a jolt and thump from the ship, it tumbled from its place and smashed against the wooden floor. Checking for a brief second that his letter to Edna was safe, he headed toward the flickering light. With arms outstretched for balance, he stomped his way to the growing flames. The *Gentle Gull*, a ship he'd voyaged in for several years, rocked and heaved over the waves of the Atlantic, lifting his empty stomach. He snuffed out the birthing fire with heavy pounds from his boot.

A bash on his mess door.

"Enter!" he said, dropping back to his seat; the sudden alert of the fire lightened his head as his heart thudded.

"Captain!"

Rain blew in as crewman Jonathan pushed open the door. His feet nearly slipped from under his bony frame. He grabbed at the knob to keep from plummeting completely.

"What is it, boy?" Fredrick said, hiding a grin behind his hand.

He had taken a liking to the lad. Jonathan was the youngest man he'd ever had on his ship. Recruited amongst a grouping of men at the docks, all he knew of the lad was that he was orphaned, with no real guardian. The grime on his face and the state of his clothes said enough. The boy was desperate for labour, and in Fredrick's experience, it was those type of men that were easiest to recruit for such voyages.

The boy had become increasingly thin and pale, and any of his innocence was drained from him with every day aboard the vessel. The horrors of slaves being forced to eat by having their mouths opened with metal brackets, deepened the shadows beneath his brown eyes. He feared most of the crew, which kept him close and loyal. On the first night, Fredrick had gotten word that the older crewmen forced him to sleep out on deck, just to see if he'd survive the night. Fredrick would have none of that. He'd threatened a flogging to whomever mistreated his fellow crewmember, and so the behaviour improved.

Rain poured off Jonathan's tattered black hat. It rested upon a head of curly black hair. His oversized shirt, once white, was torn and spotted with dirt stains, and slick with water.

"I-It's Irwin, Captain. He is calling for you from the slave quarters. There has been trouble! A revolt!"

"Is it over?"

"Yes, but—"

"Then tell him to secure the quarters and report on deck."

"No, Captain!"

"Pardon, boy?" Fredrick said, raising from his seat. His knees trembled. In an attempt to hide his frailty, he buttoned up his long coat.

"I-I think he's gone mad, Captain. H-he wants to kill

one of them!"

Fredrick pressed his lips together. Snatching his hat from the brass stand on his desk, he fitted it to his head, and staggered out. The stairs were slick with rain. Where normally he would have taken them two at a time, in his dehydrated state, he found himself taking care not to crumble at the knees. The heavy rain forced him to shield his face with his coat like a bat would with its wing. Waves assaulted the side of the *Gentle Gull*, bashing their might and drenching her deck with its icy wrath.

The carcass of the *Gull* groaned and creaked like a tortured beast. Lightning flashes revealed groups of crew members struggling with ropes, trying to secure barrels about the deck. Others battled with the lines of the mainsail, slipping and tumbling upon the deck as the *Gull* climbed up one wave and down another. Fredrick gripped a nearby rope as a whip of wind threw him down. The grind of the rusted rigging squealed as his rope held fast in its knot, and his shoulder stretched to the point of breaking as he held on for dear life. If he'd let go, he would surely have collided into a nearby cleat, leaving him a cripple, or worse. Jonathan slid to him with the agility only a younger body could offer and threw an arm around him. Upon their feet, Fredrick saw the grate of the deck, and even in the savage winds, the stench from below wafted out, assaulting his nostrils.

"Which hold?" Fredrick yelled.

"The Men, Captain!"

The grate was opened for them by two crewmen. Each gave the Captain a salute as he and Jonathan ventured down the ladder, one after the other. Thunder cracked as the storm raged on. The darkness was soon lifted by the flicker of oil lamps, dancing shadows upon the beams as they descended farther. The air was heavy and moist with bile, sweat, and human filth. The roars of the storm were replaced by the cries, moans, and screams of the cargo.

Descending the ladder, Jonathan following, they passed the first level of the hold. It was full of howling bodies. The tormented souls were shackled, crammed, seated or laying. The small space forced them to hunch beneath the beams if they chose to wander from one seating spot to the next, dragging their bloodied feet upon the splintered boards.

Further into the bowels of the ship they passed the heavily-occupied hold where the boys were stored. Screaming, their voices breaking, they trembled in their shelves. Through the rungs of the ladder was the women's hold; their chorus of moaning misery swam through his head as they reached the very gut of the *Gentle Gull*. Fredrick grabbed a lamp that hung upon a beam. Its flickering, orange glow moved across tier upon tier of the poor souls, stacked in the shelves one above the other like books. He looked up at the dozens of quivering, grotty feet, as they were always stored head first into the shelves, in spaces that were less than five feet apart. Fredrick traced a finger, following the circle of light, as though counting. The *Gentle Gull* was full, and the cargo needed to remain alive if the journey was to be his last.

Jonathan's face was pale in the horrid light. His lower lip trembled as though he was about to vomit. His look spoke a single word: *Why?*

"Their misery is not for long. Dry land, water and food will be their reward."

Leading the way, Fredrick directed the lamp to a narrow, central corridor through the shelving that housed the boys. The barrels before the passage, filled with human filth, pushed out a stench enough to burn bile in his throat. The barrels were the only source offered to the slaves to relieve themselves. Apart from the stench, the management of the younger slaves was strict, as some had been known to fall into the barrels and drown. The corridor they ventured down was mainly used by Fredrick's Clubber, Irwin. It was Irwin's task to get the slaves closer into the shelves, to make more room for others to be stored. He would bash his wooden club against the feet to get them to obey – hence his title. Fredrick looked up at the quarters as they passed, giving approving nods; they were well stocked.

"Do you think they have room to breathe, Captain?" Jonathan asked, tremors in his voice; some of the crying lads he'd passed were not much younger than he.

"You need to keep knowledge of the fact, boy, that this very vessel is one of the improved ships to grace the convoys of our trade. It is fixed with greater airflow through these bottom passages, which help the cargo survive the journeys. Much better than older ships I've worked on."

"But, the shelving, Captain. There is hardly a foot of space from their nose."

Fredrick turned, careful not to lose too much of his balance, and swung the back of his hand across the boy's pale face. "Are you questioning my management?" he said, his voice stronger than any other part of him.

"Forgive me, Captain," Jonathan said, remaining cowed. "May God have mercy on us."

"And He will, boy. This is business. I fill this ship so we need not ever take another voyage."

He took the boy's shoulder, forcing them to lock eyes. "Come, let's see to the trouble you spoke of."

Several paces down to the passage, they reached the small opening before the next set of racking which held the male cargo. A chorus of yelling and moaning filled their ears. Fredrick clenched his teeth at the sight of Irwin. This man had served loyally on two of his other voyages, but here he was gripping a bloodied slave by the head with one hand whilst holding a sword in the other. In the flicker of the oil lamps, Irwin's face was slick with sweat, the long wrinkles etched down his cheeks like deep cuts of black, and his yellowing teeth were bared behind cracked lips. His long beard, black and matted, hung like a web of dead vines and his knuckles were white and bony.

"Calm yourself, Irwin!" Fredrick stepped closer. "Tell me, what happened?"

"This savage killed Edward!" he spat, his eyes wide with rage.

"How did he get loose?"

"He undid his shackles with the fragment of a nail! He attacked Edward and murdered him!"

"Drop the sword, Irwin."

"I'm taking his head!"

"You will do no such thing! That slave is worth nothing to us dead."

"I want justice!"

"Justice has no meaning here. Only survival. Secure the slave back in his place. I order you!"

Irwin tugged at the poor man's head fiercely and brought

the blade to his throat. "Have you not the nerve to do what other commanders do in the face of such barbarity!"

"I will not entertain the act of execution. You will not persuade me."

"He murdered Edward!"

"Secure the stock and meet me on deck!"

"You are a coward! I will take this savage's head. I will show them what happens when they revolt!"

Fredrick raised his hand, which shook to the beat of his heart. Irwin was giving him little choice; mad enough to reject his orders. The stress and misery upon this voyage had put his crewmen in heavy states of distress. Disease, notably dysentery, had already taken a crewman in the first few days, not to mention a young slave, and that was before the *Gentle Gull* had even left the African waters. A deep sigh wheezed from him, thinking of the hope that this journey would be the last he would suffer. The final profit. The final time he would see any soul being stalled away like cattle. By his calculations, the coast of the Americas was still a few weeks away, so action had to be taken to try and maintain some kind of morale amongst his men.

"If you feel so strongly that a lesson must be dealt, then take the slave's foot. Cauterize the wound, then secure him to his place."

Fredrick turned to the passage. Jonathan flinched at his side when Irwin's sword fell. The clumping thud of steel through bone ate at his marrow. The screams and howls pierced their ears. As they found their way back to the ladder, Fredrick hung the lamp. Staring down at Jonathan's pale face, he said, "Do you know where Edward's body is?"

"Yes, Captain," he said, eyes downcast.

"Lead the way."

The rain was like stinging pellets against the skin. With slipping steps, Fredrick followed Jonathan past the main grate and to the door of the crewman's quarters. Upon entering, Fredrick let out a sigh of relief from the cold, yet was greeted with the lead smell of blood. Two crewmen were at work with what looked to be Edward's corpse, wrapping him in bloodied sheets in preparation for an ocean burial.

Fredrick pushed past Jonathan and cleared the rain from his face with a gritty sleeve. "Angus, Hiram, show me."

They both looked up at their captain with eyes of alarm. Rushing to their feet, they saluted. "Yes, Captain," said Angus, a tall and broad man, although his weight had already showed signs of thinning. "I-I must warn you. The savage had brutalised him."

Fredrick dismissed the warning with a wave of his hand. He had to see. There was a burning in the pit of his stomach; he'd never ordered a punishment as severe as the removal of a limb. There were the force-feeding practices he'd held by over the years, and the floggings, but it had never been this barbaric. He pressed his lips together as the sheets were removed from Edward's corpse. Sighting the body might give him some form of retribution for his judgment.

Jonathan whimpered at his side. Edward's face was a devastation, his broad middle-aged features hardly recognisable.

"Look what the savage did to him!" Hiram spat through the bristles of this grey beard.

Fredrick crouched, covering his mouth with his sleeve.

His eyes tracked the bloodied mess of Edward. Even in the glow of the oil lamps, his spine glistened through the fleshy caves of Edward's throat. His eyes were nothing but two gaping, black holes. His jaw was absent, leaving a mangle top row of jagged teeth in crushed gums.

"Whatever the savage used to murder our friend," began Hiram, "must have been thrown overboard before Irwin caught him, Captain."

"Where did this happen?"

"By the grate above the men's slave quarters."

"I want this ship searched," Fredrick said, and with the assistance of Jonathan, he pushed to his feet.

"Searched?" said Angus.

"You imbeciles! Do you really think a slave would be capable of this? Frightened and weak? There is not an implement aboard this ship that can entertain such mutilation! There are teeth marks!"

"What are you saying, Captain?" Jonathan said.

"There is a beast aboard this ship! A dog! A wild cat, perhaps? Search! Check the stores by the bow! Get every available man to arm with a blade and hunt the thing down before it claims more of us or any of the slaves!"

"But, Captain, it was the sla—"

"Silence! I've just devalued the accused slave because of this! Now find that beast!"

Fredrick snapped his eyes to the mash of flesh and gore that had been Edward's face, to see a spurt of blood gush from one of the many holes. Every man froze. All were wide-eyed as blood continued to spray. A twitch from the leg. A wriggle from the fingers. More blood. Bubbles. Foaming, rising and gurgling from the opened throat of Edward's corpse, like the workings of an old drain.

The ship churned as it rocked upon the waves, and they held onto what they could, save not to fall upon the horror on the floor. The body slid as it bled, twitching and gurgling. Fredrick shielded his face with his arm as the remains of Edward's head exploded as though shot with a hundred muskets. Fragments of bone and flesh sprayed out. Every man groaned with a mix of disgust and terror. Jonathan cried out; a splinter of bone had lodged in his forehead. Fredrick grabbed him close and plucked it free. "To the deck!" he yelled.

He froze at the door. Edward's body was not done.

"Captain?" said Angus, pointing a trembling finger at Edward's stomach; it was bloating. Like a balloon it grew, expanded.

Fredrick narrowed his eyes and clenched his teeth, preparing himself for another eruption, but not even his wildest nightmares could conceive of what took place next. With the hiss of a python, the enormous belly deflated. Breaks in the skin forced streams of blood to flow and coat the floor. From out the slop of stomach and liver, a mound rose. At first Fredrick thought it a thick bubble of blood, but it was a hard mass. The contours of its façade as it rose gave details of eye sockets, nose and a gaping mouth, frozen in a scream.

Fredrick's legs trembled. A warm stream of urine flowed down his leg and into his boot. The head continued to ascend. Shoulders, torso and hips followed to reveal a being, dark and dripping with blood. The human-like figure stood in place, its arms spread, its fingers overly-long and twisted like tree roots. Spiralling from its gut like a tangle of worms, ropes of rotten intestines were birthed. It stood at least six feet in height, towering over them all. Its bloodied face, silently screaming, looked to each in turn. Muscles and oozing tissue popped and cracked as its head ground upon a neck and shoulders that were black and rancid.

Before Fredrick could summon the strength to escape, his eyes fixed upon the moving mass within the beast's gut. Angus whimpered as the ropes of flesh shot out and weaved around his hips like a hungry whip. The crewman screamed as the belt of putrid matter tightened. Hiram stepped back, too terrified to aid his shipmate. In the orange glow of the oil lamps, Fredrick gasped as blood gushed from Angus's mouth, his eyes bulging. He turned his head as the fleshy ropes tightened such that they'd cut the poor man's body in two. Angus's torso fell one way, his bottom half, the other. Fountains of blood spurted from the dead man's stomach, his face frozen in an expression of agony.

Hiram whimpered and fell to his knees, overcome with fear. The bloody ropes found the man next, weaving around his neck. Fredrick made a lunge for the door, dragging a stunned Jonathan behind him. "Move it, boy!"

Even through the pelt of the storm, the crunch of Hiram's neck bone was clear.

The rocking deck was a chaos of rain and slipping crewmen. Fredrick gripped onto some rigging as a man swept past and fell overboard with a scream. Lightning flashed. The heavens growled. A knocking from the grate nearby. Fingers poked from the depths. Fredrick let out a sigh of horror as the digits resembled that of the monster in the crewman's cabin.

The grate burst wide.

Splinters of wood joined the hammer of the rain. The grating crashed into the entrance of his mess like an axe into a tree. A moan creaked from the ship as though feeling the wound. The vessel continued to rock with the might of the waves.

Accompanying the hiss of the rain, Irwin's screams swirled from the stinking depths. The human-like creatures climbed from the slave quarters. They were steady on the deck as they stomped out, one by monstrous one, as if their black and oozing feet adhered to the wood. The tall bodies continued to fill the deck, their guts swirling as though filled with snakes. Fredrick pulled the whimpering Jonathan with him as their backs hit the side railing. *Where are the slaves?*

"Captain! What is happening?" Jonathan cried.

Irwin was pulled from the slave quarters, screaming and struggling within dozens and dozens of the long and other-worldly fingers. Then, the intestines went to work. Like tightening ropes, they wove around his neck, shoulders, legs and waist. Irwin screamed… then gargled. Thunder boomed. Flashes of lightning illuminated bright geysers of blood. The ripping of his flesh and parting of his bones, curdled Fredrick's marrow, but what followed forced him to bite his own tongue so deeply that blood filled his mouth.

Irwin continued to scream.

He howled, his head enmeshed in the tangle of long fingers. Eyes wide, the fleshy ribbons of his neck whipped about in the rushing rain. His bellow rushed from his mouth on a gush of blood.

The monstrous beings towered, fixing their eyeless sockets to the captain and his mate. Fredrick noticed one of them carried a limp. His heart skipped when he saw one of its oozing feet was gone, cut from the ankle. The clink of chains danced about in his ears, and his eyes widened to see the shackles twisted around wrists and rotten necks. Through the storm, the other crewmen were being destroyed.

The tearing of their flesh carried on the winds.

Fredrick turned from them and stared out to the black sea. A squall of heat dashed across his soaked face. A mass of fire was burning a small distance away, rising and falling with the waves. The dark shapes amongst the thrashing orange flames showed the dancing silhouettes of familiar masts and burning sails. The odd sight forced him to lean forward, his frozen hands gripping the railing. The name of the burning vessel was etched upon a familiar bow quarter deck. The design of its figurehead, the wooden sculpture of Neptune, then wrapped with flame. The moans and thudding footsteps of the beasts drew closer. Long fingers were at his back.

Jonathan screamed. "Captain! What is this?"

Fredrick turned to his young crewman. "We never docked in the Americas," he said as Jonathan was lifted off his feet, caught in the weave of fleshy ropes.

"We are in our eternity, boy."

"Captain!"

A fingertip gouged into Jonathan's left eye.

"In life, we showed them their Hell. In death, they will show us ours."

Jonathan's screams were lost in the winds. Blood splashed

across Fredrick's face as the boy was parted. Limb from limb. He turned from the slaughter and looked upon the glare of the burning *Gentle Gull.*

Fleshy ropes snaked around his neck.

Gazing upon the angry sea, the waters carried swirling, grey bodies. They leapt from the waves like tortured dolphins. Shackles sang, and chains followed them like black tails. Some climbed the side of the ship, moaning and crying.

The ropes grew tighter.

His eyes bulged painfully in their sockets, and he wept warm streams of blood.

With vision fading to black, he had enough time to see the horrid faces of the damned.

Closing in.

Hungry.

To take their eternal fill.

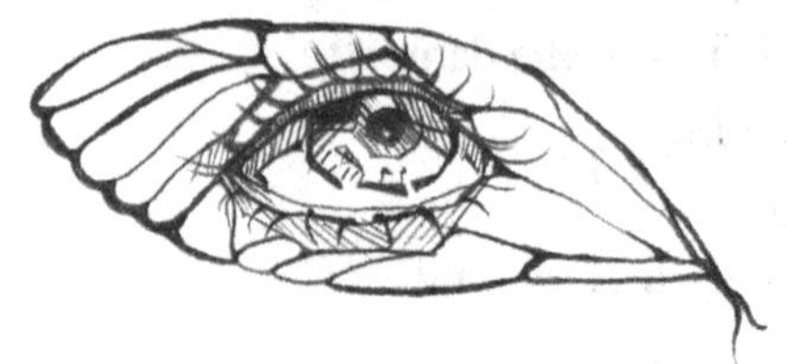

They Came from the Stars

The world as Laura had known it was dead. It'd been two years now. The surroundings vibrated around her as adrenaline pumped through her veins. Gripping the buckled harness, the muscles in her shoulders knotted with the intense g-forces of acceleration, making it feel like someone was sitting down on her chest.

Ceres, the dwarf planet, was waiting.

Laura's sight was limited, but she managed to shoot glares at the wide cabin, flickering with infrared light, her neck locked into place. Lining the walls, in three levels, were forty-nine other soldiers. Bracing. Waiting. Just like her. Shadows danced about every contour, revealing glimpses of body armour, helmets, and the vessel's arched assembly.

Every muscle in her thirty-two-year-old body tightened, toes curling within her armoured boots. The vessel's engines whined, spiralling high-pitched rings that bounced off every surface of the cabin. The piercing grew so intense, it encouraged a fight against the weight of her arms due to the enormous pressure, to cup her pained ears. However, she kept her hands where they swere, denying the impulse to grip the sides of her helmet. Others had made that mistake, struggling their heavy arms to their ears. It was a judgment call that couldn't be undone; a soldier sat across from her, head swinging between his shoulders as though his neck were boneless.

The journey to Ceres was no longer a supply mission to retrieve salt and ice for the mothership's food replication systems. No, it was a war now. Something else wanted to claim Ceres. Something hard to accept as real. Even now. Even after what had conquered humanity. Changing course to travel a year to the barren planet of Mars in search of minerals, was no choice at all.

Humanity had to fight.

Laura grimaced in her seat at the memory. Vibrations from the primary hull grew louder by the second, threatening the integrity of the landing vessel. Clasping her restraints tighter still, Laura's mind sank back to the final days on Earth.

They came from the stars.

Blocked out the sun.

Poisoned the oceans.

No one knew how many of their enormous ships cut through the clouds like tangled tree roots. The great black masses looked more like nests rather than spacecraft. Once the mysterious vessels reached the surface, the nests spewed rivers of the creatures themselves. Tangles of long, black, limbless bodies, varying from a metre long to some just a few inches, flowed into fields and streets, consuming any living being in their path. There was only one name that humankind could give the newcomers: *Worms.*

Louder vibrations.

The grind of stressed metal.

They'd penetrated the thin atmosphere of Ceres. Laura slammed her eyes shut, thoughts bent on the past: the horror of their world's consumption. When Earth's officials had tried to seek an audience and communicate, they only saw horror.

Laura was in her Melbourne apartment at the time. She'd tapped on the screen above her sink as she ripped open a package of a dried, meat-like compound to drop into a bowl. Adding water as news reports scrolled by, the brown blocks melted and formed a modest portion of stew.

The screen flickered. Images distorted. A deafening white noise. The bowl had broken onto her foot, but the image displayed on the screen had disengaged her mind of the throbbing in her toes. The severed head of the American president, Cole Foster. It was somewhat suspended in mid-air within a dark chamber—a glaring white light on his forehead. Snake-like, black organisms were twisted around his lifeless, bloodied face. They bored into his eye sockets, spewed from his mouth, wrapped around the ribboned flesh of his neck.

That's when he spoke.

Blood gurgled out of his mouth. His dead mouth. Laura's lips trembled. Her eyes dry and itchy when looking upon the horror on screen in distorted black and white.

"I don't know wh-what's happening." Foster's every word wheezed with an agony that froze Laura's blood. "I-I know people can hear m-me. I don't know how I-I know th-this. Th-they killed all the others. They have not spoken. They're unnamed. B-But the message is somehow imprinted in my brain.

"They are here, and we must not be…"

The transmission ended.

The domination of the Earth began.

A dull and heavy thud yanked Laura back to the present.

The vessel had been hit. She could picture the alien larvae bubbling on its steel. From the early studies by humanity's scientists, the larvae compound the Worms projected from their tangled limbs carried a boiling acid. An alien chemical that could reach over four hundred degrees; enough to melt lead. The thought of the vessel getting struck by such a material sent spikes up her back.

A blaring light strobed in the dark.

The hull shuddered.

Laura bit her bottom lip when the vessel plummeted, the front of the hull engulfed in flames. It had all happened so quickly.

The muscles in her back twisted when they crash-landed. Even through her helmet, she could smell her companions' cooked flesh. Her stomach churned and dived into her throat as the vessel rolled. Screams, explosions, and metal fragments shot in all directions. Whenever she caught sight of her chest plate, the more it was splattered with the blood of one of her co-fighters.

Laura screamed when the breached hull finally crashed to a halt. The interior filled with smoke. Sirens blared. Screams from the others accompanied her ringing ears. She unclipped the harness, her shoulder cartilage cracking with every movement. She staggered through the smoke and stumbled onto the surface of Ceres.

The storm threw everyone off their feet. Magnitudes of black dust and ice swirled in typhoons into the star-filled sky. She knew that craters mapped the surface, yet from ground level, they appeared more like dark-grey mountains and hills.

Laura took as much care as she could when getting to her feet, a caution not taken by the soldier next to her. He'd ripped a hole in his suit and it depressurised. All the liquid from his body was sucked out to join the howling, alien wind. Even through the background noises of death and agony, she heard the hint of his final scream.

Then…

Larvae fire. Rocketing in, catching four soldiers before her. Armor, blood, fragments of bone and clumps of gore exploded. She took cover behind the wreckage—thankful she could move all her limbs—along with survivors of the ambush.

Laura could picture the creatures' approach as she clasped her weapon to her chest; their bodies stomping forward. She peeked around the corner and her suspicions were correct. Their singular form was worm-like yet scaled and black. Hundreds of them joined together in tangles and twines to crudely form a humanoid shape that stood over ten feet tall, every edge wriggling like rattle snakes. Their larvae-weaponry fired from their tendril hands, shooting like red comets through the dark atmosphere, coming their way like a rain of certain hell.

Why? The creatures that had taken Earth, forced the exodus of the motherships into space. *Why are they here? Why this dwarf planet? Of all the places! Wasn't Earth enough?*

The vessel's carcass rocked beneath the Worms' bombardment. Laura leapt back from the wreckage as one of the creatures mounted its top, twinned arms waving in wild circles. Larvae-bullets rained. A soldier near her was hit, spotted with melting drops. He screamed, swiped at his chest plate, trying to clear the toxin but it was hopeless. His suit imploded like a crushed can, reducing him to a lump of smoking gear.

Troops prepared canons in groups of three and Laura rushed to the nearest team to offer aid. Two soldiers worked the scope and the trigger, whilst Laura had the canon shaft mounted to her shoulder. The warmth penetrated through her helmet as the canon engaged its orange plasma beam of destruction. The monstrosity was hit, and it evaporated in an explosion of black dust carried off by the alien wind.

Canon blast after canon blast, monster after monster, through the violence of Ceres' storm, the ambush was finally over. At least for the short term. She climbed to the top of the wreckage and scanned the raging landscape beyond. There were ten of the creatures, but not so close by. The pit of her gut churned to think of how many more would follow. What also throbbed in her mind was how far they'd crash landed from the war zone; a large crater at least thirty kilometres across. Would they be able to even join the war effort? Or, was this all for nothing?

She went to the rear of the vessel, battling against the might of the storm that Ceres seemed happy to deliver. Even through the rush of grey and black dust, she was relieved to see the terminal hatch was intact. Two soldiers were blocking the release handles. Their helmets tilted curiously at her as they noticed the red and yellow stripes on her shoulder: the marks of a technician. They struggled aside against the winds to allow her access. She pulled the hatch door out.

Brushing the dust and ice that immediately covered the keyboard, she tapped in the access codes to boot the scanners. The computer was online.

"Laura, is that you?" said one of the soldiers, his voice distorted through her communication earpiece.

"Barsell?" she said, not taking her gaze from the screen. "Where's Captain Harras? She was sitting near you. Did she make it?"

Laura turned to see Barsell smear off something glutinous from his shoulder plate. He held the portion of dusty sludge out for her to see. "This part of her did," he yelled.

The winds grew louder and more menacing by the second. She could imagine his African-American face knotting at its brow. She knew Barsell through combat training, and he was amongst a small group of her friends on *Mothership Hope*.

"All this for fucking salt and ice!" Barsell said, kicking at the crust.

"You know there's more to it than that."

"Yeah, I know. But why all this? Why can't we just bomb the bastards from orbit?"

"We've been over it a thousand times! An orbit blast would require a lot more plasma – we could destroy the resources we need. We have to take out the nest at close range!"

"I get it, we all heard the speech."

She didn't need to say any more. Before the war on Ceres began, the announcement was made over the PA system, which was heard on every corner of *Mothership Hope*.

"Crew. I can understand that each and every one of you fear what we are about to undertake today. I feel it too. Most of you would've already been briefed by your commanding officers, but in case the news has not reached you yet, I can confirm as your Captain, that we will engage the Worms on Ceres.

"Altering course to Mars is not an option.

"We are making a stand here. We need Ceres to survive. The Worms have taken our home world, so we will not let them take our one chance to survive in space. Let's stand strong together, and face what awaits us on the surface of the dwarf planet. Be there for the soldier next to you. Be there for your friends on this ship, and let's swat those stringy bastards into the dust."

She rapped at the keyboard. Tried to get a communication link to the mothership. "Have you done a count of survivors?" she said.

"After the ambush? I'd say there's just a dozen!"

Barsell flicked away the last remains of their captain and looked over Laura's shoulder. "Can the mothership hear us?"

"No. The link is offline."

"What about Cadence?"

"What?"

An icy wash coated her face; Cadence was her partner. She worked on the bridge as a navigation technician. "Why would Cadence hear us?"

"Weren't you both working on a link unit? You know, so you could communicate with each other?"

Laura rested both hands at either side of the console, more to settle herself. *Why did he have to mention Cadence?*

It was hard enough leaving her for the last time, accepting the reality that they'd never see each other again. Ever since the transport launched from the shuttle bay, the memories of Cadence were clouded by the events of every millisecond.

The landing.

The blood bath of the Ceres surface.

Battling with the console and trying to get some sort of status. And then, here comes Barsell mentioning Cadence as though they were about to hook up with her in the mess hall.

She needed a moment and stepped back, the thunder of Ceres rumbling beneath her boots. Months ago, when first seeing the images of the dwarf planet, it looked so peaceful and quiet. She wouldn't have thought it would nothing close to that. Ceres was an angry world with a singular, harsh raging storm. Thoughts of her partner flooded to the front of her mind. Distracted from the hell around her, she let them come. Laura hadn't been a soldier then. She was a woman. A heartbroken girl. Her memories traced back to that first day on the mothership, on the training deck.

"That gun is probably not the best choice," came a voice over her shoulder as she was about to collect a large, black rifle from an armoury rack.

Laura turned her head from the scope to find a woman in uniform. Slightly taller than herself, perhaps a touch thinner, her green eyes sparkled against fair skin, and her long, black hair combed over the left side of her skull revealed a fine buzz cut. Red lips held a smirk.

"No offense," the woman said, "but I was watching you take that rifle off the rack like it was something you've never seen before."

"We were told to grab a weapon and shoot the targets,"

Laura said.

The woman let out a small laugh. "That's fine, you're just trying to obey orders. That's what we all have to do. But, I do believe the sergeant wanted you to grab one of the phaser pistols from the rack on the other side of the deck."

The woman pointed across the floor to the large gathering of trainees lining up to be presented with their issued pistol.

"Oh shit."

The woman laughed again. "It's ok, you're not the only one, believe me." She held out her hands to accept the rifle.

Laura handed it over as though she were handling a viper.

"You've got a good eye, though," the woman said, gesturing the weapon. "This is one of my favourite pieces. Light, super accurate, and good for holding off the Worms . . . but, it will kind of burn that nice face of yours right off your skull if you're not wearing a visored helmet."

Laura racked fingers through her short, blonde hair, blushing with embarrassment. "How the hell would a gun do that?"

The uniformed woman tapped at the glowing amber capsule on the side of the rifle. "After you press the trigger, inside this glowing chamber is a fusion of charged particles, broken away from helium atoms, which transforms tiny bursts of heated gas into plasma. Think of having a miniature sun right next to your face. That's why you need a helmet and heavy gloves to use this bad boy. The barrel gets pretty hot."

Laura looked away, heart thumping and feeling like a moron.

"Hey, don't feel bad. Everyone here is learning. We'll

make a soldier out you, Private. What's your name?"

"Laura."

"Private C. Mass. But, you can call me Cadence."

She shared a smile, one Laura would come to long for at the end of each day. "I best get over there for a weapon that won't melt my face off,"

"See? You're learning already,"

"Now, I've got to come to terms with the fact that we'll be flying into the asteroid belt."

"Why are you coming to terms with that?" Cadence said, giving her a curious look.

"Flying into the asteroid belt doesn't sound like a bad idea to you? The whole squad I'm assigned to are freaking out about it."

Cadence stepped a little closer, lowering the rifle to her side and resting on it as though it were a cane. "You don't know much about space, do you?"

"Not really. I used to build computers, not read about the solar system."

"Well, let me put you at ease. When you think about all the movies where asteroids were drifting about in an unpredictable chaos, smashing into each other? Well, the real thing in comparably spacious. Even though there are billions of them out there, the closest distance between two of them is about one million kilometres."

"I guess that's why they call it *space*, eh?"

"You said it, Laura." Cadence smirked. "So, rest easy. We're safe from colliding with any big potatoes out here. Share that with your scared squad buddies, alright?"

"I'll make sure to mention it."

"Catch you later, Private Laura."

Laura was shaken back to the present as Barsell gripped her shoulder.

"You ok?" he said over the winds.

She nodded.

"Look, I'm sorry I brought her up. I know you guys were close. I just thought, you know, maybe?"

"We did work on a device, but it was just a fool's hope. It doesn't work, the distance is too huge."

"I'm sorry, Laura,"

"You can be such a dumb arse, you know that?" She placed a hand over her chest plate. Beneath the armour rested the small device no bigger than a thumbnail. It dangled from a thin chain along with her dog tags. Again, her mind wandered…

…"It's finished?" Laura said as she turned the small, copper-coloured tube in her hands.

"As much as it can be. I sealed it up after my shift. Mine's done too," Cadence said, pulling hers from beneath her singlet. She clicked the end with her thumb, and a small beep alerted from both of the units. A tiny red light flashed on each of them too. Laura looked at hers in wonder.

"Go ahead," Cadence said. "Say something."

Laura's heart raced and she hesitated with the little, flashing communicator. She bit at her lower lip as she brought it to her mouth.

Cadence brought hers to her ear in eager anticipation.

"I don't want to go," Laura muttered.

The small smile Cadence wore had vanished. She walked to the door of Laura's quarters, holding her device to her lips. "I'm going to go for a walk, you stay here," she said into her piece.

Laura held back tears to hear Cadence's voice through the small unit in her fingers.

The door opened and Cadence walked out. "Let's just talk like this for a bit. Pretend that you're down there and I'm up here . . . talk to me,"

"I don't want to waste our time. Please come back."

"You're not following the rules, Laura. Pretend with me. I'll come back, don't worry. Just talk to me. You haven't spoken much since you got drafted for the supply mission. Talk."

"I don't want to leave you."

"I don't want you to go."

"There's nothing else," Laura said; she was talking through tears then.

"Yes, there is,"

"I'm angry, ok? It feels like suicide!"

"This isn't war, this is survival. And you're allowed to be angry. I'm angry too. I hate that you've been drafted. I know it's not fair."

"I'm scared."

"You're allowed to be scared. You'd be an idiot not to be. But, you know what?"

"What?"

"You're a good soldier. I'm not just saying that because we're close. I'm telling you how it is."

"It won't matter with those things, those Worms! No one has come back!"

"I know it's no picnic, but some that don't come back

are fighting in the crater down there. It's not because they're dead."

"Please just come back?"

"I'm already back."

Laura lifted her head to see Cadence at her door. She stepped in, the door hissing closed behind her. She rested down on her bunk and whispered, "Lay with me."

Laura did, taking her usual place close to her side, resting her head on Cadence's warm chest, hearing the beat of her heart. Feeling the tips of her fingers as they ran through her hair. She wept.

"Nothing is fair. We just have to face this," Cadence whispered.

"The communicators won't work. The range is—"

Cadence held her communicator up before their faces, allowing it to sway like an old clock's pendulum. "It doesn't matter. They're a piece of us now. We've spoken through them. Just us. That's what matters. But the only way you're going to survive down there is that you stay strong. You're a good fighter. I've seen it in training."

Cadence glided her hand down Laura's face, smudging her tears. "Even the strongest will can achieve anything. Be strong for me. For us."

Laura reached for her warm hand. Fingers interlocked, palms pressed, they drew each other's faces near…

"Laura? Hey!" yelled Barsell.

She shook the thoughts of their kiss from her head.

"What do we do? Can you do anything?" he howled again through the winds.

Her ears rang and her gaze swept back to the console.

Sparse green lights appeared on the flickering screen, which were promising. "The local beacon is still working," Laura said, stepping back in front of the terminal. "At least I can try and find out where the fuck we are. Maybe we can make contact with one of our units in the crater. They might send out a transport!"

"How far away is the zone? Can we make it on foot?"

She ran a scan and the software produced an aerial image of their location. "Two miles."

"Running two miles in this fuckstorm?"

"I know," she said as she turned her head in the direction of the lurking creatures beyond. "We wouldn't make it ten metres with those fuckers this close."

"What do we do? This bird won't fly anywhere."

Laura studied the image. A scream blared from nearby. Canons fired.

"Worms!" a soldier called.

No technician on any mothership could explain why the Worms never showed up on their scanners. No one saw them coming two years ago when they arrived on Earth, and there were no alerts to tell them that the Worms had a nest on Ceres before they started their supply missions.

Barsell lifted his weapon. "I guess we stay here and fight 'til the last soldier. We don't know how many Worms are between us and the battle crater."

"Wait," she said. A dark-blue form displayed on the screen, near their position. "A hundred meters. East," she said, stabbing a finger at the screen.

"What's that?"

"There's another vessel! It's bigger than ours. Much bigger.

A tanker."

"A tanker? They came down in the first wave. That was a year ago. Is it in pieces?"

"No. There's a damage detection alert, but it's together."

"I guess we're sprinting there then."

"There's one more thing. I've got life readings."

"You're fucking with me, right? Survivors for that long! How is that possible?"

Laura gripped her weapon. "Let's go find out."

Laura lifted the canon barrel from her shoulder and launched forward. The soldiers behind her gathered the other components and followed. It was the process. They advanced a few meters against the onslaught of the storm, Laura crouched, the canon was mounted, and the blast was delivered, evaporating another tendril-engorged monster into oblivion. She drew a deep breath before every surge forward, eying the three other teams doing the same. The tanker was a dark blur before them. Swirling screeches came from behind. More of the creatures were coming. They were being surrounded. The winds were assaulting with such force, her legs were beginning to buckle.

We're dead.

They were all going to suffer the melting agony of the alien's larvae. Sinking through their armour like hot coals and cooking their flesh. When she made to grasp Cadence's beacon, a glint caught her sights.

A light flashed from the tanker.

A rocket shot through the storm, over their heads and into one of the creatures. It exploded in a mash of mangled, alien gore.

"Run! Don't stop!" Laura yelled, pushing through the wild gusts as though she was running against the waves of a shallow surf. She knew all too well that the rocket damage to the alien was temporary. When blown apart, the creatures had the ability to form again into their crude, toxic, twined images. A resurrection of sorts. This was why the disintegration cannons had been developed.

She eyed the soldier holding the rocket launcher in his hands. He was before an opening at the tanker. If they were able to miraculously survive this alien environment, it would be because of this loan survivor. Their saviour didn't seem to fear the creatures re-emerging behind them and fired again over their heads. His rocket waved a red, blazing trail though the wild dust storm, and connected with another giant tendril form. The creature exploded with a screech.

The soldier hastened them, gesturing with his large weapon. The creatures were closing in. An alien projectile tagged a soldier nearby. Laura watched him die through the blur of the storm. His chest exploded forward, and his legs folded in opposite directions, causing him to slip in his own remains. They all made a break for it. Her team was closest and was the first to make it to the safety of the tanker. The steel panels of the floor smacked hard on her chest as she crashed in. The sudden absence of the howling winds forced Laura's head to swim. More of the other teams stumbled in, collapsing to the floor on their knees or face-planting like herself. Their rescuer screamed through his visored helmet—"*Get in! Get in!*"—as the final stragglers dived from out the raging outdoors.

The door slammed shut like a metal mouth. The floor rattled beneath them and they were left within the dull hum of the tanker and bathed in the blue glow of the security lighting.

Depressurising steam filled the chamber, the hissing piercing their ears.

"Who did we lose?" Barsell yelled, gripping the sides of his helmet as the steam began to thin.

"I think it was Tory," said Laura. "He was our only medic."

Their saviour stepped inside their circle, his boots thudding on the grill of the floor. "Lucky for you that you're now inside a tanker." Unclipping the side of his helmet, he lifted it, revealing wrinkle-webbed face. A scar ran down the side of his forehead, and his fair hair was long, and wet with sweat. "This tanker was the first to withstand the onslaughts of the enemy's toxic snot. The air is safe in here, too. So, let me see your pretty faces." He grinned through thin, cracked lips.

Barsell was the first to unclip. Laura and the others followed suit. She took a breath and coughed. The smell was rotten. Stale. Rank, like the bowels of a sewerage pipe.

"There, that's better," their saviour said. His gaze fell on Laura. "Speaking of pretty faces."

His eyes were pale, his skin pasty. He took a step closer and she held firm. "It's been a year since I've seen a woman." The back of her neck itched as his beady eyes looked her up and down, pausing at the mounds of her breasts. Then, his eyes fell on the coloured stripes on her shoulder. "A technician, too? This day is getting better and better. Although, that buzz-cut doesn't do you any favours."

Barsell stood, stepped forward. "Thanks for helping us back there. Now, how about you tell us your name?"

The saviour laughed from the back of his throat. Laura grimaced at the man's rotten teeth. She inched back.

He regarded her again, noticing the lines on her face bend with alarm. "You don't have to worry about me, sweetheart. I'm so covered with warts downstairs, I scream like fuck whenever I take a piss. I couldn't do anything to you even if I wanted to."

"Your name?" Barsell commanded, stepping nearer.

"Well, before that," the saviour said as his eyes glazed down to the green stripe on Barsell's sleeve. "How about you all tell me who is the ranking officer amongst you? I know it's not you, Private."

They all looked at each other. Laura's heart pelted a little harder as the rescuer's eyes fell on her again. "You look to be out-ranking every one of your followers, being a technician. So, you should be asking the questions, not him," he said, stabbing a thumb at Barsell.

"Alright then," she said, straightening. "Who the fuck are you?"

"Corporal Burak. And who might you be, soldier?"

"Laura, sir," she said and saluted. "That's Barsell. The others are—"

"Nah, we can get acquainted later." Burak dismissed her with a wave of his hand.

A hatch opened at Burak's feet. Another soldier climbed in. He was big and broad. Bald, and a long straw-like beard.

"Here's a member of *my* crew. This is Cadan."

The brutish soldier regarded them with a nod. "Wow, company? You all look like shit," he said as a smile formed within the bristles of his bread.

"Cadan, this is the new party. Take them to the rec room so they can catch a breath and clean up. Bring them to the bridge after that. Then we can share some food and get properly acquainted."

"Sure. This way, you lot!" he said, gesturing with a swing of his arm towards a circular door that rolled itself into the steel wall cavity with a deafening grind.

Laura's unit glanced at each other, confused. Steel fixtures on the walls screeched and creaked. Pounds of impact thudded as though being bombarded by a hail of boulders. Every soldier braced, looking about.

"You nervous lot," said Burak with a huff. "I'm afraid that noise comes with this hotel. Don't worry, though, the Worms won't get in here. The shields have plenty of life in them yet. Now, get yourselves cleaned up. Wipe some of that shit off your armour. We're about to brake some hydrated bread together, so I don't want to be staring at a smeared eyeball when I'm feasting, okay?"

One of the soldiers, a young Russian, noticed the eyeball on his own shoulder plate and jolted.

"See? Go with Cadan and he'll take care of you."

"Come on, children," Cadan said. "It's bath time before dinner."

The unit hesitated and looked to Laura for direction. "Let's just do it," she said. "Then we can eat. He did just save us."

The mountain that was Cadan lead the way, and when Laura motioned to follow, Burak put a hand on her shoulder. "Not you. I need you to check out a terminal on the bridge. You can clean up later."

Barsell stabbed a gaze at her over his shoulder.

"Is there a problem, soldier?" Burak said to him.

"How do we know we can trust you?"

"You don't. But try and relax. Mummy will be waiting for you."

"Just go, Barsell," Laura said.

"That's a protective soldier you have there," said Burak, laughing again from the back of his dry throat.

"Can I accompany you, sir?" Barsell said, his brow determined.

"Just go," Laura said, annoyed. "Go and clean our captain's guts off your chest and we'll meet up in a minute. It's cool, I said."

Burak laughed from his belly. "What was your captain's name?"

"Harras, sir. Captain Jane Harras," Barsell said.

Burak rubbed at his slimy chin. "Harras, huh? Can't say I knew her. But, I'm sure she wouldn't appreciate one of her soldiers wearing her blood like a fragrance. Remember, I outrank the lot of you, so get yourself cleaned up, that's an order."

Barsell obeyed.

"Alone at last. This way, Soldier."

Laura didn't move and Burak stabbed a look.

"With all due respect, sir. I would appreciate a moment to clean up. I'd then be able to provide my full attention."

"Look around you. Do you think I have any fucking powder rooms around here?"

"All crafts this size would have a few stationed latrines, especially near the bridge. It'll just be a minute. I take it that you've all survived because of the filtration systems?"

"Drinking our own recycled piss was part of it, but there are other factors."

"Then the water is in good supply. If I could just have your permission, sir. Five minutes is all I need,"

"You've got two."

Laura closed herself in to the small latrine. It reeked of human waste and the temperature was enough to make her sweat. She looked down at the small sink, spotted with brown mould. Turning on the tap, she cupped some of the warm water and splashed it on her face. Her eyes were sealed shut. Her mind reassuring her that the water was safe – the process had an 87% efficiency rate, water was pumped and extracted, salts were separated from acids… *It's clean. It's clean…*

She wiped her face dry with the underside of her sleeve and worked her fingers through the chest plate. Fishing out the beacon, she dangled the little device before her face; she wanted to try, she had to. It was all she could think about. Would Cadence hear her? Thumbing the button, her heart thundered as the light flickered.

"Son of a bitch, it's communicating," she uttered.

"Laura?" a crackled voice replied. "You survived the

landing? We had reports the vessel crashed."

"It did. Only a few of us found shelter. We're in a first-wave tanker. It's been here for—"

A rapping at the latrine door jolted her.

"Two minutes are up!" Barsell yelled from the other side.

"Coming, Corporal Burak!" she said purposefully into the device before tucking it back behind her chest plate.

Bathed in the crimson glow of the power-saving lamps, the bridge rested before her. The foreboding gloom was accompanied by a pulsating hum, expanding and contracting at the back of her heart. Two monitors glared on the far side, but every other terminal on board was dead.

The generator at the tank's core must be on its last legs, not to mention the oxygen supply.

Burak brushed past her and led the way to the terminals. He stared at her. "You look a million dollars. It's amazing what a gal can do in two minutes."

"What can I say, I'm resourceful. And fuck you by the way."

He laughed and nodded. "I like you, Private. We gotta have a sense of humour in this shit-arse situation. You have permission to laugh and shit-stir me all you want."

Laura smirked, hoping that her communicator was operating, and that Cadence and anyone else was listening. She could only hope they would be silent and were able to track their position; perhaps decide to send aid. She squinted through the gloom at the terminals beside Burak.

"Yeah, I know what you're thinking. We're low on power, but there's a backup generator on this turtle and I need you to access it. I've tried to the point of wanting to blast a fucking whole in this console. I need *you* to fire it up."

The steel walls vibrated, creaking every bolt.

The Worms.

"You'll have to get used to that, like I said before: the fuckers are all around us, bombarding this shell with their toxic shit. The shields have held, but time is running out." Burak pointed at the terminal in a gesture for her to get to work.

Laura seated herself at the terminal. The system was older than those she was familiar with, but she was able to get into the mainframe and locate the backup generator within minutes. Her heart skipped as the matrix had provided nothing but white noise.

"Good news or bad news?" she said, accessing the structural reports of the tank.

"No generator," he murmured, as though to himself. "That's the bad news, right?"

"Correct, sir."

"Then what's the good?"

"The damage readout on the tracks of this tank are repairable. We could get this thing moving again. How many of you are there?"

"There's five of us left. But there were twenty who survived the original crash. They've since fallen to disease or to the Worms."

"Well, sir. With *us* here, you now have enough manpower to make repairs. In tight shifts we should be able to correct the malfunctions at night."

"How long would you expect the repairs to take?"

"I'd have to officially assess the damage, but according to the reports…" She tapped and scrolled through a page of data, illuminating tables and rotating three-dimensional structural drawings, all with a small scatter of red flashing dots, indicating the troubled areas. "It shouldn't take more than a few nights, give or take."

"This unit came with some spare track treads, rods, and welding kits. The Track Hatch is still sealed, too."

"Okay, that's the small access point to the outside. We'll need to access it to do the repairs. We'll be vulnerable as the shields are not protecting that hatch, even now."

"What did you say?"

"It must be due to the power supply, sir. The sooner we get the tank moving, the better."

"No shit. I didn't make corporal for nothing. I have a plan. And that involves *not* repairing the tracks."

He leaned forward to the keyboard. The stench of salty sweat and rotten teeth made Laura's eyes water. He tapped away, breathing fluid-filled breaths, as though the process excited him.

"Look," he breathed from the back of his throat.

The screen displayed an aerial view. He tapped a few more times, enlarging the image out towards the north.

The nest.

She squinted, amazed that the image was captured. "How is it possible that we can see their breeding hole? We could never detect them from orbit!"

"I put it down to the human attack line. The amount of

canon fire that's heating the area every day has had an impact on the thermal imaging. It's managed to capture hints of the Worm's nest. The weaker part… We're closer than you think."

"What good will it do, sir? I mean, being this close to the nest. We need to be at the front. Help advance the position, so we can get the disintegration canons in range."

"Ah, but you're not looking closely enough."

She peered at the screen as he enlarged the image of nest. Although the picture was dated a year ago, and only in tones of black, green, and grey, she spotted an enormous bulge at the rear of the nest. "Is that—"

"Correct. The sack. It's where the human attack lines can't get to. We're in a position to come from the rear. Even with our hand canons, we can penetrate it. It will slow their reproduction and give the front the time they need to get in range."

She looked up at him and he leaned back, staring down at her. "Sir, if I may, we could try focussing our effort to get mobile and make contact with the mothership. This information is invaluable. If done right, we could arrange an offensive to attack the sack with a lot more firepower."

"And waste more time?"

"We can't achieve this alone, I'm sure you know that,"

"Incorrect, Private. It's achievable once you accept it's a one-way trip."

"It's doesn't have to be."

"It's war. Sacrifices are required. We need to do what has to be done. Like back on Earth. Humanity needed to put survival first over being wiped out by an enemy it couldn't defeat. So, the same applies here, millions of kilometres away, but this time is different. We fight, not run."

He crouched down so that their eyes were level. "We need to be creative, find better ways to survive, get back to instincts. You know the boys that got sick after we crash landed here? They needed better care I couldn't provide. The food simulations on this tank wouldn't cut it for the human body, especially when it's damaged. Those machines weren't designed to produce sustenance that would be consumed for long periods of time. Those boys needed nutrients, natural food. Protein. Vitamins. But, it's war. I need to do what's necessary to get the job done. I know you know this, but it's good to get some perspective. Now, turn around. I want to show you something else on the screen."

When she faced the monitor, she was too slow to stop Burak's sweaty arm from wrapping her into a chokehold. She gripped his forearm and tried to claw at his face, but his hands were fast, slipping beneath her chest plate and gripping the communicator. A sting pinched the front of her throat as he yanked the chain free of her neck. She glared at him as he stepped back, swinging the little, flashing device before his face. He thumbed the button and Laura's heart sank to see the tiny lamp flicker out.

"I told you; I didn't make corporal for nothing."

"It's just a communicator, sir. I have made contact with the mothership. We can try to receive aid—"

"And get rescued? Is that what you want, little princess? To have some horses trot in and carry you away into the sunset? You think this tiny little device is gonna achieve that? I picked you for smarter."

"It's not about rescue, it's about following through with

your plan with the least amount of casualties."

"Oh, but that's not *my* plan. I don't care about the casualties; I care about wiping out the enemy. The greater good. The few for the many."

He crouched again. "We are acting now before the Worms start to populate the side of this rock. We can't sit on our hands and wait for any cavalry. We're on our own, so stand up and face it."

Her eyes fell upon the device that dangled on its chain from Burak's sweaty fist.

"You want your toy back?"

"It means something to me."

"Oh, really? I can respect that. Here," he said as he twisted the device before her face, detaching the button, along with its tiny globe with a crack, and dropped it in her hands. "Knock yourself out."

She gasped as an icy sweat beaded her forehead. "Fucker…"

"I haven't changed my mind, Private. I like you."

A door hissed open. Cadan stepped in with Barsell and the others in tow.

"Well, it looks like the party's here," said Burak getting to his feet. "Don't worry," he said down to her. "You'll learn the rest of my plan when we brief your unit. I know you think I'm nuts, but it'll make sense. Trust me."

The bridge was soon full in the gloom, heavy boots shuffling in and around the main table. A surface that was once heavy with monitors had since been cleared. The rest of Burak's men had also arrived. Two were younger soldiers, but the other was broad like Cadan, his dark-skinned face mapped with scars, as though he'd once used a nest of razor wire as a pillow. They all looked to be well nourished despite being stranded.

All this from hydrated bread?

A trail of spikes went up her back when she realised that her unit was no longer armed. Their heavy battle shields were removed, leaving them with their standard uniforms. Burak's men, however, were still clad inside their heavy gear.

"You all going somewhere?" Laura couldn't help but ask as she tucked Cadence's communicator back beneath her chest plate.

"We're at war, Private. We're always ready, even when we go to sleep."

"Yet my team look as though their going out to dinner."

"Well, they are! Besides, their armour had obviously required a good hosing. Is that right, Caden?"

"Yes, sir. Their gear sure caught a lot of shit out there." He smirked through his scars.

"Well, if your done quizzing me, can I introduce the rest of my crew?" asked Burak.

"Why not… sir."

"Good. The two young guys are Pete and Morak. The big fucker over there is, Dylan."

All nodded their greetings whilst Pete and Morak tossed an assortment of foil-wrapped packages on the table along with a stained steel canteen. The rumbles from outside rattled the tanker's shields. Laura could sense the unease on the faces of her unit, but Pete, Morak, and Dyan were unmoved.

"Go ahead," Burak said. "Help yourselves. Rip them open,

add some water and eat. Don't worry about the Worms. Like I told you, they won't get in. It's just white noise to us."

The unit hesitated. The last hour consumed their minds: the chaos of the landing, the struggle to survive the surface, and now the stinking hold of the stranded tank.

"Fuck this, I'm eating," said Morak. He had a whiny voice, as though it hadn't broken yet. He leaned over the table, snatched a package, and jostled with the wrapper with grotty fingers.

"Why are you lot so stiff?" Burak asked through a laugh. "Well, I guess you did just get shot out of the fucking sky. Come on, grab your share. This is all we're getting today." He turned to Laura. "Eat up, Private. I'll get you and your crew up to speed."

"Affirmative," Laura said with contempt as she picked up a package. "This is what you survived on for a whole year? Bread?" she asked. Her gaze caught Barsell inching his way to her.

"We ration it. Along with the filtered piss," Burak said, reaching over the table and grabbing his portion.

"What's the plan?" said Barsell once he got to her side.

"Our position is closer to the nest than we thought," she whispered to him. "The corporal has a plan to attack it from behind."

"The sack of the nest is exposed," said Burak, directing his eyes to him. "We only need to hit it a few times to puncture it. Your fancy canon will do the job well." He splashed water over the hardened compound of yeast and flour. It grew from the table into a modest, grey bun. He grabbed it and took a bite. "It's two miles away," he said, chewing.

"Sounds like a suicide mission," said Barsell. "We won't get within range. It'd be crawling with Worms, sir."

"We?" Burak said. "You got it wrong soldier. We can't all go. Sixteen soldiers trying to cross this surface undetected? We may as well be a herd of fucking elephants." Fragments of grey mush sprayed from his mouth. "There can only be the five of us going. Light. Quick. The Worms might not even notice our approach until it's too late. Then we blow that sack and give our frontline a chance to burn them down. Then the motherships can continue their supply mission so humanity can grow potatoes fertilised in their own shit. Mission accomplished."

Laura tilted her head, perplexed. "So, what will the rest of us do here? Monitor your pathway? Warn you of the Worms?"

"No. You all have a much more important role to play. It was a real gift you all got shot out of the sky, bringing that new canon with you. Makes this plan possible. Better still, you're all going to give us the strength we need."

A slicing sound cut the air.

Gasps and gurgles.

Throats were slashed and blood sprayed in every direction. The bubbling and the splashing of blood echoed. The thud of bodies hitting the floor attacked Laura's ears as though she was being paddled with a slab of wood. A sharp, stinging sensation exploded from her gut. Her face felt like ice, as though she'd been thrown into a freezer. She coughed blood. Her eyes dropped down to see the glint of a long, steel rod.

She'd just been run through.

The taste of lead filled her mouth. Her body trembled.

She inhaled as the rod was withdrawn. A hand gripped her shoulder, keeping her upright. The slaughter before her continued, Burak's men hacking the heads off the remaining members of her unit with skilful, two-handed blows. Barsell lay face down on the table, already dead, stab wounds to his back.

Dylan turned Barsell over, his limp arms falling like dead snakes. His eyes, white and vacant, stared up at the dark. His mouth was wide in a frozen scream and his teeth were red. Laura gripped her own gut wound, blood pulsing from between her fingers with every struggled heartbeat.

"Do you want to know how we survived out here for this long?" Burak said close to her ear. "It wasn't just the rehydrated bread and recycled urine."

Even in her final moments, she had to suffer the rancid odour of his breath.

He spun her around and stared at her with his grey eyes. "Nah, you see, it's so fortunate for us that little lost units like yours fall from the sky. All scared, unaware and fresh." He licked his lips. "Such a vital and free source of protein."

A roar of a motor whined and echoed off the walls. Dylan had started up a circler saw, one normally used to release soldiers from wreckages. The large, silver disc of the cutting blade turned before her eyes as he guided it to Barsell's corpse. The whining lowered in pitch as it ground into his stomach. Laura twitched as her blood drained, her heart in her ears. Lips trembling, she turned her gaze away as shiny blood sprayed over Barsell's vacant gaze.

She gagged as Burak's hand clamped around her throat. "Thank you for your sacrifice," he said, letting her down and taking a step back, unsheathing a dagger.

He casually swung, slicing her tender throat. A cold and sharp pain. The warmth of her blood spurted out and she choked, eyes bulging.

"It's a waste, to tell you the truth," he yelled as he cleaned the blood from his blade on his sleeve. "I did have a mind to spare you, but you look too delicious, darling."

Her vision toggled in and out, and she fell back onto the table next to Barsell, draining. Twitching. Her anger pumped with her pain and rapid breaths. The deafening whine of the saw hovered over her. She tried to raise her hands to Cadence's broken communicator, but they failed to obey. Laura thought of the curves of Cadence's face, the strands of her dark hair over her eyes like a perfect curtain. Her smile.

Laura was still alive when the spinning blade sank into her stomach.

The hardest part of being dead was accepting it.

Laura had seen people die many times. She'd watched with watering eyes as her younger sister Tilly was crushed by the ceiling of their home when they'd tried to escape the fire engulfing the building. Down the hallway they sprinted, Tilly just a few strides in front. Laura could remember the nausea as she trailed behind, the smoke shrouding her sight, scratching at her eyes. The coughing. She'd wished she was blind when she thought of what happened next. The ceiling came down in a merciless instant. Laura stood with the settling dust and heated smoke in the seconds that felt like hours. Saw the lifeless face of her sister, her skin powdered with dirt, blood, and dust. Wide eyes staring at nothing. Body covered in broken plaster, splintered wooden beams, and bricks. The blood pool growing larger from beneath her head and shoulders.

That was when the Worms came.

The larvae bombs had dropped.

Buildings had crumbled.

After that, witnessing death became a regularity. Even when she'd managed to board one of the motherships, being far from the invaded Earth, death was there too. It followed in dormant viruses that some citizens and crew thought they'd conquered back home. Anything from herpes, varicella, and cytomegalovirus, became evident. But new illnesses had birthed and mutated. It had taken several dead before the sicknesses could be contained, managed, and finally treated.

Now, it was Laura's turn to be in death's embrace.

But why the agony?

A million razors sliced beneath her skin.

Her teeth, dry and gummy in her mouth, ached with coldness as though frozen. She drew a breath and her chest rattled as if it was full of gravel. She couldn't feel her legs, her hands, her toes. Nothing but the agony of the spikes beneath her flesh. She made an effort to move her head, but her neck was fused, glued in place. The dark, angry sky was violent above her.

Forcing as much strength into her neck as possible, she tried to look down at her chest. But, it wasn't there.

Her breaths were laboured and rapid.

How am I breathing?

Rocks shifted around her. Fluid-like movements slithered about her ears.

Worms!

Thousands of them.

Everywhere.

Her vision rocked as she was tumbled and dragged on the alien surface. She caught sight of the tanker, only yards away.

They discarded me! Dumped me like garbage! What they didn't eat, anyway.

The Worms were taking her, dragging her within their tangled, toxic, and slithering river.

"Laura?" a voice wheezed through the bubbling, squelching larvae.

Barsell?

His head was slick with blood and membrane, rolling about amongst the moving, wormy twines. His eyes were wide and bloodshot. "How are we alive? What th-the fu-fuh?"

"The W-Worms," she managed before her head rolled into a blob of warm, tar-like slime and then resurfaced. "They're re-regenerating. Forming again. We m-must b-be caught in the—"

"We're gonna be p-part of one of them?"

"D-Don't know . . ." she managed between gurgles of black slime.

They rolled and tumbled about amongst the alien forms, drenched in the larvae that would normally melt their flesh. However, they were part of the Worms now, at one with the slimy, slithering consumers of life, caught in their regenerative flow.

The Worms sucked her away, higher from the planet's surface. Laura's eyes rolled as she was raised up the mound of twirling, black tendrils. Barsell's head gathered in the build, rolled up and followed her pathway.

Ceres's stormy landscape of sharp rocks and hills was clearly in view. The tanker before them was being whipped with violent dust. Two other Worm forms had birthed at either side, their tendrilled arms outstretched; long, warped, root-like legs taking heavy steps forward. Laura knotted her face, not to the wriggling agony beneath her skin but to try and communicate to the monstrous form she was now at one with. Willing with every ounce of thought she could muster, she clenched her teeth, longing for something to move to her will.

A mass of the wriggling tentacles glided before her face and stopped at her nose.

Just like she'd told it to.

Turning her eyes from it, she realised she'd commanded the right arm to raise. Her jaw throbbed, her teeth unclenched, and the huge arm dropped. Gasping, now rocking her head from side to side, she tried to command other portions of the form, other limbs. Nothing moved. The right arm twitched, but that was all.

"What a-are you d-doing?" said Barsell from just below her.

Drips of thick saliva hung from her mouth as she looked down to him. All she could see was a portion of his face. He was lodged in the form's chest. She realised she was higher, mounted perhaps on the left shoulder.

She coughed out a glutinous, hot mass of yellowing larvae before speaking. "The arm. I could move the a-arm. You try and move something. Try the legs."

"All I feel is pain, like my brain is being e-eaten!"

"Try, for fuck's sake! Think of them as your own!" She spat more sludge then commanded the right arm and it flicked up, knocking Barsell across the forehead.

"Did you do that? Why aren't we dead?"

"Just try! If I can, so can you!"

Barsell whined and groaned through his teeth.

The form rocked and swerved.

The landscape before her tilted.

The tank zoomed closer.

"You're doing it!"

Barsell screamed, half in agony and half with elation. "I'm doing it!"

The tanker zoomed in again.

Closer.

"What are we going to do?" he said, gargling larvae.

Laura lifted the arm. The tendril-hand rattled like a mass of angry snakes. Larvae birthed: dripping, oozing, forming. She growled through her frozen teeth as the mass expanded. Hardened. "Let's pay the dinner party a visit."

Laura's larvae canon melted the track hatch like hot coal on ice. Clumps of orange steel dripped from the opening. Barsell commanded the legs to advance them forward; he was learning quickly through every scream of misery. This new machine they commanded, this new vessel, was a house of unspeakable spikes and burns beneath whatever of their flesh remained. Laura's eyes were bereft of moisture, and she could imagine razors slicing across her vision with every second. Her eyelids were sealed open, and her sight was blurry at best.

Even through the smog of her sight, she scoped down the corridor to the bridge's entrance. Forms of Burak's men stood in attack position. Bright flashes erupted. Gunfire cracked from down the corridor. Again and again, bullets came at their wormed vessel, rapidly hitting their enormous form. There was no extra pain from the impact of their kinetic projectiles, which felt like nothing more than meaningless vibrations. Barsell moved the great legs, one pounding step at a time. Laura ground her teeth again, forming new larvae in the monstrous hand.

She fired.

Screams surged from down the corridor. Barsell gurgled a yell and took them into a run. They burst onto the bridge, their great arms flailing like that of a wild bear. Sprays of larvae showered the room. More screams came as the burning, alien acid found their marks, melting flesh. Laura snapped her head from side to side, not interested in Cadan, Pete, Morak or Dylan as they dived for cover. She pushed out a roar through her teeth as she sighted down on Burak squirming beneath a desk.

Barsell stepped the form towards Burak's cowering body, his face smeared with blood. One of his eyes had melted in its socket. A hand trembled away from his jaw. Half the flesh to his cheek had been burned away, revealing black, rotten teeth and gums.

"Look up, fucker," she gurgled.

He lifted his gaze, his pained face contoured with horror. "Private? Holy shit, you looked fucked up," he muttered, blood spitting with every word.

"Time to admire you're handiwork," she said, forming another mass.

"Let's just hold off a second," Burak coughed. "We can still work together. We have an advantage if you're passing as one of them!"

A crash and squeal shook the grounds of the tanker – two other Worms from the outside had joined them. Charging onto the bridge, their large arms waved and lashed in wild thrusts. Whips of larvae shot into the gloom like machine gun fire. Morak and Pete were caught in the toxic rain, the cabinets they hid behind offering no protection. Their bodies steamed as they were cooked on the spot, larvae passing through uniform and tissue. Dylan lunged and screamed from a corner, fumbling with the disintegration canon. The nearest Worm, almost casually, fired its larvae. Dylan's large body exploded like a balloon. Cadan attempted to crawl out of the bridge, his legs melted away to the knee joints. A Worm stomped on his crawling body and its tendrils expanded from its arms, wrapped around his head and tore it off with a crunch.

"Let's talk about this, bitch!"

She fired the mass into his cowering form. The squeal that came from his bloodied mouth caught her ear for a brief instant, and along with the sharp and stabbing pains that bit at her face, she felt gratification.

She'd reduced Burak into a scatter of blood and bone.

Her eyes readjusted to the outside world, the dust storm. The intertwined Worms expanded and contracted like rubber bands as Barsell roared them into a sprint. Leaping over the sharp, rocky landscape, they advanced as fast as they could.

The nest was nearby.

Other Worms, in their human-like forms, contorted as though curious, when Laura and Barsell rushed past. The thump and flash of the battle lit their path. They needed to get close enough, to get in range, to complete their final push.

The surface of Ceres vibrated. Other Worm forms were in pursuit; they'd been found out.

"J-Just a little farther," Laura gasped. "J-Just one sh-shot!"

Barsell screamed as their speed increased.

Laura broke her bottom lip as she bit down, enforcing her command of the entity. Tendrils twirled around the disintegration canon she'd retrieved from Dylan's remains. Her vision was spotted as the Worm bodies around her head began to consume, to burrow. Her hold on the vessel was breaking, it was claiming her. It knew she was an imposter, a threat. Barsell's screams diminished into great choking coughs as he was digested. Enormous strides had turned into stumbles as his lifeforce was extinguished.

Laura choked. The vision to one eye was obscured.

Cadence's voice spoke to her.

Even the strongest will can achieve anything.

Laura fired the canon with her last ounce of life. The final hints of her sight were covered by a veil of black fissures.

Boom.

Even through the tiny lines of her vision, the great sack of the nest was punctured. Reproductive sludge poured out in black rivers.

Multiply now, you bastards…

She managed a grin before the darkness swallowed her.

The Great Invocation

A tired gramophone labored as chorusing trumpets and piano scratched from its needle. It blared into the small auditorium thick with the scent of tobacco and aged wood. Harry Mogadino pranced onto the small stage, the tails of this dark coat dancing about his legs. In the glare of the lights, he gracefully presented a hand toward the back of the stage. On cue, his faithful fox terrier, Benny, ran out into the spotlight, his frilly white collar bouncing with every padded step. Harry tapped the breast of his coat, and Benny leapt into his arms. Synchronized to the scratchy music, The Great Mogadino threw up a white-gloved hand, Benny let out a high-pitched bark, and the two awaited their applause.

One could hear a pin drop.

Harry glanced around the auditorium. His heart sank. Only a dozen or so pale faces were scattered about the seats.

The music sprang back into life, jolting him from his gloom, and he let Benny down so they could perform their first trick.

Benny ran to a box, and clamped an alarm clock between his teeth. Harry tapped on a small table and Benny trotted over and set the clock upon it. Covering it with a small black cloth, Harry looked towards the pitiful audience. Sighing, he turned on his heel and flung the cloth away. In time with the recording, the trumpets blared *ta da!* to reveal that the clock had disappeared. Harry tapped on his breast, Benny leapt into his arms, and they appealed for their applause.

Cough... Cough...

The rest of the show was torture.

Harry's spirits were deflated, but there was always hope in Benny. His wagging tail, and his little panting mouth suggesting a smile. He'd never changed. There had been good times once; performing inside packed houses. Yet even though times had darkened, Benny didn't. He was the bright light in Harry's life, always devoted, always loyal.

The final chorus resounded over the auditorium. The audience gave a scattering of claps and coughs.

Harry groaned as heavy crimson curtains dropped, leaving them in a cloud of dust.

Benny licked at his cheek. The frill of the little dog's collar pinched at Harry's neck, and he couldn't help but chuckle as he eased him down.

"You've lost your touch, Mogadino," said Cordel, the theatre's owner.

"It was a tough crowd."

"Crowd? I've seen more folks line up for the latrine!"

"So, I won't see any commission for tonight?"

Cordel laughed then puffed from a cigar and said, "You don't fill theatres no more, Mogadino. Face it, you're finished. Let the younger showman take over."

"I'm only thirty-five!"

"There are folks ten years younger doing a better job. But they won't be seen dead in my rat's nest. You should think about pushing a broom!"

Harry lowered his head to Benny. "Up boy, time to go."

He tapped on his chest and Benny leapt into his arms once more.

"Don't come back, Mogadino. Another goon showed up this morning asking for you. I don't want no trouble around here!"

Harry said nothing as he removed Benny's frilly collar, and stepping out into the street, he let the cold breeze carry it away.

Harry and Benny's single-bedroom apartment was nestled in lower Manhattan. On the fourth floor on Fifty-Second Street, Harry fumbled with the locks before pushing the door open. Benny raced onto a pile of tangled blankets—his makeshift bed. He nestled himself into it, facing out to view Harry's whereabouts.

"Sorry there is no dinner," Harry said. "I'll check the fridge, but it looks like we'll have to settle for some old apples,"

"I understand," said Benny, in his little, gruff voice. "Could I trouble you for some water?"

Harry stepped over and gave him a pat behind the ears; Benny always loved that. "You don't have to be so polite. Face it, I'm a horrible provider."

"It's not your fault, Harry. You're trying. We'll get through this the way we always do."

Harry huffed out a small laugh and went to the sink to fetch a dish of water. He crouched and watched Benny lick it dry. Benny looked up at him, his tongue flapping around his muzzle, catching the water that had collected around his whiskers. He panted, showing his undying smile. Harry gazed at him lovingly. Benny's head was mostly black, but for the small wisps of tan that brushed above his eyes, giving him a constant look of concern.

"Does it discomfort you to talk?" Harry asked. "I would hate to have given you a curse."

"Of course not, Harry. It was strange at first, but it has become easy. My thoughts, as you know, haven't changed. I'm just able to speak them in your tongue. I think it's a gift."

"Indeed. But I don't know how long it will last. I acquired the spell in Europe and it didn't come with instructions."

Benny stared. "That's not what troubles you though. I see it in your eyes."

Harry scratched Benny behind the ear and said, "The guilt will always be there."

"You're only human. Stop punishing yourself."

Harry crossed his arms as he always did when the foreboding shadow of self-hate crept up his shoulders. "It wasn't for the want to hear you speak that urged me to seek council with those cultists. It was greed. *The World's First Talking Dog!* I'd already had the posters drafted. I can't believe that it had to take our sinking ship, loosing money and years of sets and equipment, for me to see that. When we docked in New York on the rescue boat, we were left with nothing but the clothes on my back."

"And my voice."

"Which will never be sold. I was a fool. The show was doing well and we were set to retour Sweden. Yet, I was so easily seduced to sell your voice to packed theatres across the eastern seaboard."

Harry retreated into the kitchenette. "You've been given a bad deal, Benny. A money-hungry illusionist, and now a struggling showman that can't even feed you. Not to mention the debt. I owe my family a great deal of money,"

"Are you finished?" Benny trotted from his bed and sat at Harry's feet, looking up at him and cocking his head. "Do you think me *that* shallow?"

"Shallow?" Harry crouched to him. "I've taken you for a fool. I would deserve your abandonment."

"Do you know that canines never fall in love instantly? Love is earned."

"All I've ever done is work you to the ground and plot to use you. When have I ever earned your love?"

"I was a puppy. We lived in that nice place overlooking Central Park. You came home one day to find I'd torn your leather loafers into ribbons. You were cross, and you sent me to bed. But you never hit me, nor did you yell at me. You just cleaned the mess. You didn't stay mad at me for too long. You called me over, patted and fed me. Life went on as normal. That was so important for me."

"Why?"

"You've had many friends in your life—all I've ever had is you."

"That's a pity."

"I have no regrets," Benny said, and put a paw up on Harry's knee. "You are my friend."

Harry jolted as a rapping at the door echoed through the apartment. Benny's ears stood to attention. They shared a glance.

"A bit late for visitors," grouched Benny.

"Go to the bedroom. I'll close you in. You'll be safe,"

"Safe from what?"

Harry got up. The door was rattling violently.

"In the bedroom! Now!" he whispered harshly, stabbing a finger at the door by Benny's bed.

Benny lowered his head and trotted off. Harry stepped over to the door, but when he looked back, he saw that Benny had settled into his blankets and was staring at the door, growling lowly.

Stubborn boy!

Harry unlocked the door. "Hold on! I'm opening up!"

The door inched open and Benny let out a high-pitched bark when a heavy fist met Harry's jaw, knocking him to the ground. Three men in dark suits filled the room and slammed the door shut behind them. All wore fedora hats with rims draping shadows over their eyes.

"On your feet, magic man!" ordered one of the goons. He then turned to one of the others. "Shut that mutt up, Paul!"

Harry's heart skipped as the largest of three men stomped over to Benny. He jabbed the side of his shoe into Benny's muzzle and yelled, "Shut up, you little rat!"

Benny hurled backwards with a yelp, then charged at Paul's leg, sinking his teeth around the foot of his trousers.

"Hey!"

Harry cringed when Benny yelped again. Paul had belted him with the side of his firearm, and aimed it at his head.

"No! Don't!" Harry cried, getting to his feet.

"Hold it, Paul!" the goon nearest him said; he looked to be calling the shots.

Paul lifted his gun as Benny continued to bark.

"You kidding me, Stefano? That little mutt just tore my trousers! I just bought them!"

Stefano turned to Harry. "Shut the mutt up. Now."

Harry leaned toward Benny.

"Benny! Stop barking!"

Their eyes met.

"Listen to me," he pleaded. Benny did so and sank into his blankets, growling up at Paul.

"I could have shut that thing up with one bullet," said Paul. "Now it's growling!"

"The boss wants them both," Stefano said, stepping up to him. "You kill the mutt, then the boss won't have anything to bargain with, *capiche*?"

He smacked Paul's hat off, revealing a head of shiny, black hair parted to one side. "You gotta lot to learn, you schmuck. Get that mutt on a leash."

"There's no need. He can come with me. He's well trained," Harry said, eyeing Paul as he collected his hat from the floor.

Harry tapped on his chest. Benny ran and leapt up into his arms.

"Don't go trying anything funny. I was told to deliver you both alive, but that doesn't mean in one piece, got it?"

Harry nodded and they all proceeded out. Benny tucked his little head into Harry's neck.

"I'm sorry. You should have gone into hiding," Harry whispered to him.

"I'm no cat."

Aless paced impatiently below the marble staircase. Classical music drifted in from the main lounge of his uncle's mansion. The chatter of countless attendees rumbled like a distant railway. Everyone in the family was invited to seek a final audience with the great Philip Bonano. Aless had his hands berried deep into the pockets of this dark blue, pinstripe pants. He lifted the rim of his white fedora when he noticed someone coming down the stairs.

"Alessandro, your uncle will see you now," said Joseph, his uncle's private butler. He stood over Aless holding a silver tray.

"It's about god-damn time!" Aless spat, stomping up the stairs.

"Not so quickly, Alessandro. There is a condition to the visit."

"What?"

"Your dear uncle, on his death bed, demands that all visitors have a taste of his true passion before entering."

"What the hell does that mean?"

"You must indulge in one of your uncle's delicacies before proceeding upstairs."

Joseph offered up the tray.

Aless looked down at the single item and tried not to retch. "I gotta eat that slop?"

"To reject this is to reject your uncle's heritage. It was caught fresh this morning from the fishing business founded by his great-grandfather. He grew up with these delicacies, the foundation of the empire. All must honour this if they wish to see him."

Aless sighed. He hated oysters. Raw, cooked, or otherwise—but what choice did he have?

He collected the single shell from the tray—Joseph looking on in anticipation. Aless pinched his nose with thumb and forefinger, grimaced, and took in the oyster with one gulp. Then he coughed loudly as the slimy thing slid down his throat.

"Very good, Alessandro. Was it delicious?"

He spat into the shell with disgust, slammed it onto the tray, and stormed up the stairs, his shoes clapping on the marble.

He stepped into the dimness of Phillip Bonano's grand bedroom. A nurse busied herself with a small basin and cloth at his bedside, and his Auntie Gianna walked up to greet him.

"So good of you to come, Alessandro."

"Auntie," he whispered, and they greeted each other with a peck on each cheek. "Can I speak with him?" he said, removing his hat.

"For a little. He's very weak."

Aless nodded and stepped slowly to the bedside. His auntie ushered the nurse away with her. Uncle Bonano was breathing noisily. His silver hair was not in its usual neatness. His wrinkled cheeks, usually shaved smooth, were covered in white and grey bristles. Cataract eyes looked up at him.

"Alessandro?" he croaked. "Did you have an oyster?"

Aless gulped. "Yes, Uncle,"

"How was it?"

An itch crept up his neck—his uncle knew he hated

them. "Like all oysters. Cold and slimy."

Uncle Bonano croaked a small laugh. "Alessandro, you have never changed. You were always the nephew that wanted the prize but never thought to appreciate the game. You hate fishing, yet you eat fish?"

Aless sighed again. "I don't understand what you're saying, Uncle, but we still haven't settled some business. I was hoping—"

"That's right, Alessandro. You've never understood!"

"Phillip?" Auntie Gianna said from across the room, hearing her husband's raised voice.

"Uncle, please," Aless said, leaning closer. "That heist uptown. I gave the tip. Everyone had gotten their share of the diamonds, so where's mine?"

"You little schmuck! Open your eyes for once."

"What's going on here?" Auntie Gianna marched over to the bed.

Phillip let out another croaky laugh.

"Nothing, Auntie. Uncle here was just about to finish some business by telling me where—"

"Business?" Auntie Gianna snapped. "Have you no heart at all, Alessandro? You have to leave!"

She gripped his arm.

"Uncle? Tell me!"

Philip's croaky laugh grew louder.

"Leave!" she demanded.

Aless eased back. "As you wish." And with that, he stormed out.

Waiting for him at the foot of the stairs was Stefano, his hands deep in the pockets of his long, black coat.

"Hey, boss. How was your meeting with Mr. Bonano?"

Aless stepped to his right-hand man and snapped, "I hope that old fuck dies the most painful death ever! I hope he vomits up his own shit!" he said, stabbing a finger up at the marble stairs.

Stefano just nodded, then leaned close. "Boss? We got him. Just like you asked."

Aless stood back and raked fingers through his hair to settle his temper. "And the mutt?"

"Yes, boss. The boys have them in the basement of the old man's garage. No one will hear a thing."

Aless straightened his jacket. "Let's do this."

It was quite a regal room for being beneath a garage, but one would expect no less from Mr. Bonano. Harry stood upon an elegantly weaved rug with Benny still trembling in his arms. The room was draped with crimson and had all the workings of a private club. There was a pool table, and in the corner was a bar with mirrored shelves filled from floor to ceiling with spirits and wine.

Harry eyed his captors. They were scattered about the room, either smoking or sipping whisky. He jolted as Stefano entered, followed by someone he hadn't seen since he was a teenager.

"So here he is," Aless said, stepping in and lighting a cigarette. He took in a deep drag, then smoke streamed out of his nose and mouth.

Stefano shut the door. He stood with Aless, their black

shadows stretched out over the rug. "The magic man, huh?" Aless said, taking another drag. "Remember me, cousin?"

Harry gulped. "Of course."

"How long has it been?"

Harry had to think. "I'd say it was before we were eighteen?"

"That's a long time. I know we're far from close, but family knows family. Time for a reunion, don't you think?"

A shiver of fear raced up Harry's back.

"We've gotta talk, cousin. But first, you gotta lose the dog."

"What?"

"You can make this easy, or we can make this messy."

Harry looked over Stefano's shoulder to see one of the other goons bring over a birdcage fit to hold a parrot.

"That's Vinnie, by the way. He likes hurting things."

"My dog will be fine with me, I assure—"

Benny let out a deafening yelp as Stefano gripped the scruff of his neck.

"All right, here!" Harry cried as he released Benny. The look in his little dog's eyes drove daggers into his heart. "Easy! Don't hurt him!"

Stefano fed Benny into the cage and shut the door. Benny's little high-pitched bark echoed. Vinnie stood over him, nudged the cage with his foot and yelled, "Shut up!"

"Hold on," said Stefano, peering at Harry. "You gotta make your mutt keep quiet. Do it again and Vinnie cuts out his tongue."

Harry called out, his hands open with appeal, and sure enough, the barking stopped. But Benny stared up at Vinnie, baring his little teeth.

"Now we can talk, cousin," Aless said, taking another drag of his cigarette. "Do you need a drink?"

"No."

"Suit yourself." Aless snapped his fingers and called out over his shoulder. "Paul! Whisky—no ice!"

Harry watched as the big brute delivered the drink. "You look to have fallen on hard times, cousin," he said, taking a sip.

"So it seems."

"Well, *you're* the one that strayed from the family business. When me and the others were playing with G-Man guns, you were reading weird books."

"I wanted to be a showman, not a crook."

"Look where that got you. Right, boys?"

Their mocking laughter filled the room.

Harry froze, his gaze fixed on Benny in his cage. He was looking out at him, his small eyes screaming: *Get us out of here!*

"You got some nerve. We're businessmen, not crooks. We lost track of you when you went off to be a circus act, then what do you know? You and your dog are up on posters all over town. Doing big shows and making loads of bread."

"That bothered you?"

"Of course. Out of respect, you owed Philip Bonano a share," Aless shrugged. "You don't understand how our world works. Before I got the chance to teach you a lesson, you go and disappear again. Off abroad, right?"

"I wasn't aware I was in debt then."

"It's worse than debt—it's disrespect! Then what happens? You come back and grovel like a weasel for cash? You got some balls, cousin. I was shocked you didn't get whacked on the spot. I couldn't believe my uncle loaned you a dime! What did you do, hypnotize him?"

"Your mother and mine were cousins. They were close. He pitied me, I guess."

"That's right—the shipwreck. Lost everything apart from that mutt over there."

Harry nodded.

"The cash you owe the family is over three grand. It's paynight, cousin."

"I just need more time, Aless."

Harry's heart skipped as Stefano stepped up and punched him across the chin. He fell to the rug, landing hard on his side, his head spinning. Benny was just a blur in his cage, barking constantly.

"Get him up!"

Rough hands lifted him from under the arms. Paul closed in and fired a punch into his belly. Harry gasped for breath.

"That's enough," said Aless.

Stefano let him go.

Harry staggered, clutching his gut, and Benny only let up barking when his master shot him a look.

"Just a little taste, cousin," Aless began. He stepped up to him. "You gotta big problem here."

"You just need to give me some more time. I just need a few good shows and I'll have the money," he said, rubbing at his bruised stomach.

"You got no money hiding in a bank somewhere? Did it all go down with the ship?"

"I have funds in a bank in Europe. I initiated a transaction before I set for home. I received a cable from the bank telling me it had failed. It's all still there. I just need to make enough funds here so I can open an account and recover the money into it!"

"How much are we talking about?"

"At least fifteen hundred."

"Only half, cousin? That won't make your problem go away. But what if I told you that I, too, have a problem. Maybe we can help each other out?"

"How?"

"I need your magic."

"You mean my illusions?"

"No."

The smile vanished from Alessandro's face. He stepped close, too close for Harry's liking. "You do more than that, and I know it. Do you think the family is stupid? They kept their eyes on you in Europe. You moved a large sum of cash to a private buyer."

"It was fraud!"

"Bullshit! Sources said that you met up with some strange folk and bought something from them about a month before you set sail for New York. When I finally got the job of dealing with you, I dug a bit deeper, see? They were Latin, those folks. Religious. I heard all sorts of stories, and I don't know what to believe, but what I do know is that you bought something, and it has to do with spirits. You learned how to call them—how to make them do things."

Harry paused, his eyes darted back and forth from Benny to Aless. "You're wasting your time. It was a hoax. It didn't work."

"*What* didn't work?"

"What I paid for. It was a stupid move and it cost me."

"Lies, cousin. If whatever it was didn't work, why were you in such a rush to come back here? Your shows were doing well abroad. Why tour here? Why?"

Harry couldn't find any words, his mouth opened and closed, but nothing came out. His jaw ached.

"I thought so. You *did* learn something from those priests. You know how to rouse the spirits."

"Even if I do, what then?"

"I've lost something, and I want you to call a spirit to find it. Did you hear about the big jewellery heist uptown?"

"No."

"Well," Aless scoffed. "That operation was based on *my* tip. Those diamonds are worth millions. Everyone got their share but Uncle Bonano is yet to give me mine. He just feeds me riddles."

"You're talking about me using invocation to summon a spirit to find your loot?"

"That's what I'm talking about. Or there's another option." He snapped his fingers. "Vinnie?"

Benny yelped as Vinnie booted the cage.

"Stop it!"

"You see," Aless began, stepping up to Harry and forcing him backwards. "We could always gut your mutt, then put you both in a box and make *you* fucking disappear! That's *my* kind of magic."

"The only spirit capable of finding missing things is a demon. That's what you want me to try and bring into this room?"

"Vinnie!"

The flick of pocketknife cut the air and Vinnie began to kneel.

"All right! All right! Stop! I'll do what you say! I'll try."

"There you go!" Aless laughed and patted Harry hard on the shoulder. "It's all you got, cousin. It's all you got."

Sweat beaded on Harry's brow. His requests were met—a table, the leather-bound notebook he had tucked in his coat, and an assistant were made ready. All the while, Benny barked from his cage.

"Could I ask for one more thing?"

"What is it?" Aless asked, not hiding his impatience.

"Could you please give me a moment alone with my dog? I can make him stop barking."

Aless stared down at Benny. "Two minutes. If it doesn't work, the mutt gets it."

Harry ran to the cage and took Benny to the bar, where they were left alone. Benny's barks turned into whines as he set the cage on the counter top.

"You need to be quiet," Harry whispered.

"I'm scared," Benny ruffed. "They want to kill you."

"Our only chance is for me to perform the ritual."

"How do you know it will work twice?"

"I don't."

"Please be careful. Did a demon really do this to me? Give me a voice?"

He gulped before answering. "Yes. But don't worry

about that. Worry about being quiet. You must promise me. Whatever you see from now on, be silent. I don't want them to hurt you. Promise me, Benny?"

He nodded his little head.

"Say it?"

"I promise I will be silent."

"No matter what they do to me. Understand?"

Benny nodded again.

Harry returned Benny to the rug. Resuming his place at the other end, he rested his hands on the table and looked up at his assistant, whose shadow inked over the table.

"Why did you choose me?" Vinnie asked, his bottom lip flapping over his upper like a bulldog's.

"Because you're the most gorgeous, meat bag!" yelled Paul.

Laughter erupted.

"You want a knuckle sandwich, fuck face?" Vinnie bellowed back.

"Easy!" yelled Aless. "Let's get this show on the road."

As the laughter died down, Vinnie addressed him again. "Seriously, why me? I don't want to be a part of your circus act."

"Because you're the one with the knife, and I need you to cut off one of my little fingers."

Benny let out his high-pitched bark and Harry stabbed a finger at him and pursed his lips. Benny whined and cowered in his cage.

"What the fuck?" said Aless.

"It's necessary," said Harry as he slipped off his coat.

"I'd gladly cut anything off you," began Vinnie. "But you telling me to? Kind of takes the fun out of it."

"This is not about fun."

Harry unbuttoned his cuffs and rolled up his sleeves. "The ritual demands an offering of the flesh,"

"Wait a minute," said Aless. "If you've done this before, what else have you cut off yourself?"

"A toe from each foot."

Harry opened up his small book and flipped through some pages.

"Mother of God, this guy's a fucking freak," Vinnie said, taking a step back.

"What's with all the mutilation?" Aless asked.

"I didn't pick you for squeamish."

"Screw you, cousin. I just want to make sure you're not trying to pull any funny business. Spill it! Why the finger cutting?"

"I'm not a true worshiper of Satan. I'm an intruder, inviting a demonic spirit into our world. I must offer a piece of me as a gift. I'm making my finger sacred. If this pleases the spirit, it may, in return, provide its services."

Aless let out a sigh, rubbed his brow, and looked at Vinnie. "Do what he says."

Harry placed his right hand on the table and spread his fingers. Vinnie flicked out his pocketknife, the blade glinting in the amber glow. He gripped Harry's wrist with his free hand and brought the blade to the centre knuckle of the little finger.

"Not there," Harry began. "As close to my hand as you can. The whole finger. All of it."

"That's gonna be tougher to cut through. It's gonna hurt like hell."

"That should please you then."

Without further hesitation, Vinnie pressed the blade into the flesh.

Harry grunted as the crunch of bone pierced his ears. He squinted as Vinnie rocked the blade until the little digit came free, blood squirting. He snatched a handkerchief from his pocket and covered the burning wound, trembling and channelling the pain by grinding his teeth.

"You best back away now," Harry groaned. "I'll take it from here."

Vinnie looked at him as though staring at something unfamiliar, then took a few steps back. Harry looked at the handwritten verses in his notebook. Sighing, he dipped a finger into the pooled blood and smeared an upside-down, five-pointed star enclosed within a circle upon the table's surface. He then looked at Benny, cowering in his cage with paws over his eyes. After clearing his dry throat, he allowed the Latin verses to roll off his tongue:

I conjure thee, spirit, to come and show thyself in fair and comely shape without guile or deformity by the name of Casmiel! By the name of beloved Lucifer! Find and bring forth the treasure we so longingly seek! By the dread day of final judgment! By the omen! By the changing sea of glass! By those beasts having eyes before and behind, and having one hundred hands! Seek, ye holy one! Seek!

Harry made a fist of his good hand and looked to the ceiling.

"Is that it? Is it here?" Aless asked, looking around as

though trying to track a fretting fly.

"Don't interrupt. I'm not finished," Harry hissed and continued in the loudest voice he could muster.

I beg you, ye holy one! Regal and majestic! Glorious splendor! Mighty arch-daimon! Denizen of chaos and Erebus, and of the unfathomable abyss! Haunter of sky-depths! Murk enwrapped, scanning mystery, and guardian of cults! Flame-fanning terror darter! Heart-crushing despot! Satanachia of daimons! Invincible Lucifer!

The silence deepened.

All the men looked at each other. Aless dropped his cigarette butt and snuffed it with his heel. Harry's heart raced, and the burning in his wound shot spikes up his arm.

"I have to hand it to you, cousin," Aless said, reaching into his coat. "You had me for a second, thinking you could actually do that, but it looks—"

"Wait!" Harry yelled. All of his flesh goosed and he felt a familiar chill. His knees began to wobble and his heart thudded harder. "It *has* worked! We are in the presence of the divine. It will appear. It will seek your prize,"

"Really? How will it appear?" Aless said, his voice almost bored. He pulled out his revolver and pulled back the hammer with a click.

"Do any of you feel different?" Harry asked, looking at them in turn. "The spirit has come through, but not in its true form. It should be in one of you!"

"I think we all got a bit of the demon in us—right, boss?" huffed Vinnie.

Laughter. The rest of them revealed their firearms.

"Vinnie?" Aless said, pointing his pistol down at Benny's cage. "Shoot the mutt first."

"You got it, boss."

Harry trembled where he stood, his eyes wild as he watched Vinnie step over to the cage.

What's happening? The sensations were the same as last time. Where's the spirit?

Vinnie aimed his hand canon down at Benny, only to hesitate.

A growl—deep and throaty, as though from a tiger.

"Boss?" Vinnie said, staring down. The growls continued through bared teeth. Vinnie shook his head as though to shake away cobwebs.

Harry could swear Benny's teeth were getting longer.

"What the fuck has gotten into that mutt?" Aless asked, looking at Benny's eyes, which Harry could see had transformed into black orbs.

Vinnie started circling the cage, and Harry watched as bulges rose and sank around Benny's muzzle—was he growing?

"Put your guns away," Harry said. *Of course*, his mind raced, *the spirit has come through a vessel that has received dark magik before. Like a familiar plane!*

Benny let out a deafening roar. His fur had begun to sprout like a rash of spikes about his back. His canine teeth grew down to dreadful points.

"Vinnie? Shoot the mutt!" Aless said, taking a step back.

Before Vinnie could pull the trigger, Benny's size had reached the limits of the cage and he broke through as though it were built of cardboard. He launched himself at Vinnie's broad throat and sank his newly-formed teeth in. The big man gurgled as razor jaws worked into his flesh like a meat shredder. He fell hard on his back and trembled as the blood fountained from his jugular.

Benny whipped his head back to Aless and growled.

"Holy shit!" Aless tried to shout, but it only came out as a terrified whisper.

Benny stepped over the trembling legs of the dying Vinnie and stalked Aless. Blood and saliva dripped from his fangs and gore hung from his paws.

Harry stumbled back and Stefano fired a round, but Benny lurched out of the way as though seeing the bullet in slow motion. Stefano kept firing but the blood-soaked canine swerved past every bullet and—running with unnatural speed—launched itself. The powerful jaws clamped the hand that held the gun. Benny ripped Stefano's arm from its socket, leaving a geyser of blood in its place. Stefano screamed and fell to his side.

Paul fired next, only to miss his mark and catch Stefano through his left eye. He fired again and again, and Benny ran for the nearest wall. Defying gravity, he raced up and over the ceiling like a spider, then dropped onto Paul's shoulders. His curved claws gripped bone and his maw expanded abnormally. The razor teeth bit into the top of Paul's head.

Paul wailed and his gun fired shot upon shot in all directions, forcing Harry and Aless to drop for cover. Harry cringed when the cracking of Paul's skull cut the air. The shooting ceased and Paul froze, his eyes wide and his mouth wider still. Blood poured from beneath his hat and covered his face—the final curtain.

Benny kept growling, baring his teeth and Paul's legs finally gave out. He collapsed with a thud.

Benny raised his head, thick blood stringing from his jaws, and his black eyes fell upon Aless again. The beast sprang, canine limbs twisting at impossible angles, and Aless fired helplessly before being knocked to the ground.

"Cousin! Call this fucking thing off me!"

Benny's muzzle dug into Aless's stomach.

"I don't understand!" Harry yelled. "It should be searching for…"

Harry crawled away from the table and looked on in horror as both his dog and his cousin thrashed around on the rug. Alessandro's suit was growing bloodstains upon its jacket and trousers. Benny's growl had become gurgled and Aless let out a squeal. He was on his back, the canine perched on his pelvis, his jaws ripping at clothing and flesh. Aless punched Benny but to no avail. His attack slackened and his arms soon flopped like dead snakes.

Harry retched as he watched his possessed terrier feast upon the gut of his second cousin. His brow raised as the beast dug profusely at intestine and liver. Chunks of flesh and gore travelled out from between his hind legs, the way dirt would if he were digging for a bone in the earth.

Harry cocked his head, seeing that Benny had clasped onto something. He watched as Benny withdrew his muzzle and backed away, then dropped a morsel of flesh. He sniffed, pawed, and licked away at it. When it was clean, he picked it up with his teeth and trotted over to his master.

Harry fell to his knees to meet Benny, but the dog

stopped short, dropped the morsel on the floor, and froze. Harry's heart lurched as Benny let out a woeful whine and shrank back to his former size, bones snapping and flesh shrinking before he collapsed to one side.

"No!" He took Benny in his arms and cradled him. "Benny! Benny, no!"

A bloodied cough escaped the little dog's mouth and he whined. Harry hugged him tight, crying into his blood-soaked fur. He hadn't lost him after all.

"I'm so sorry, my friend. Are you still with me?"

"Let's...go home?" Benny croaked.

"Yes, Benny. It's home time. I'll get you cleaned up."

"Harry? Don't forget what is at your knees."

He eased back. Grimacing, he picked up the clump of flesh with his good hand. It was still warm.

He allowed it to settle in his palm, and his eyes widened.

He paused, tilted his head, and sniffed.

A large diamond.

And it smelt like fish.

Festive Creatures

Dark Tales of Christmas

When All Goes Cold

Shane stared at the bars of his cell. Although it was freezing, he sweated; Division D had that effect, especially at night. He looked at the other bed; Fondo was lying there. Of all the nights to be celled with that prick, it had to be the last night of his six-month sentence. Shane just wanted out and to be with Tracy for Christmas Day. She loved him and accepted his faults. She was his rock and he longed to be home with her in their one-bedroom flat. He *had* to change. No more auto theft and pub brawls. Now, all he needed to do was survive Christmas Eve.

He faced Fondo. "I'm staying awake, you know."

"Aw, but Santa won't come."

"What did you do? Pay one of the guards to get in here with me? If you've got a present, then try and give it!"

They both stood; Shane clenched his hands to fists.

"Now, now," said Fondo. "Be good for Santa. It'll be cleaner that way."

"Try it like a man. I fucked you up like a man when you wanted me to suck your cock, remember?"

Fondo swung his makeshift knife. Shane ducked and weaved, catching Fondo with a left hook across the jaw. A sharp pain struck Shane's bicep as Fondo's blade went for his throat. Shane landed a head-butt, knocking Fondo out. Shane collapsed, panting. His head throbbed as though struck with a brick.

The air grew colder.

Footsteps forced his gaze to the bars. He struggled to his feet and staggered over to see. Through the gloom, there was someone descending the stairs. It was a tall, obese man.

Silhouetted.

The shape of him suggested that he wore a bristly beard and a heavy coat. Shane's heart skipped when the man paused; the sight bored into his marrow. Goose flesh formed on the back of his neck. His teeth felt like ice and his breath formed clouds. The man was looking at him. Into him. Shane jolted when the figure turned and stomped back up. His heavy steps signifying solid boots with metal soles. Shane watched as darkness swallowed him.

He'd heard ramblings here and there about Division D – a large man in black. A past prison doctor, some inmates would tease. He'd appear when blood was spilt, or even before. Yet Shane's brain argued that it was his throbbing head playing tricks.

Shane dropped his pack and caught Tracy in a hug. He looked toward their Kingswood, idling at the curb, billowing smoky petrol and burnt oil. He gathered his pack.

"Nice to have you home for Chrissie Day, babe," she said.

Shane gave her a peck on the cheek and turned to the prison. Out over Division D, in a window of the tallest building, stood the man. Staring down at him. Into him, icing his cheeks.

Tracy motioned to the car and he snatched her hand. "What's up, babe?" she said.

"Sorry, we can't risk it, Trace. We're taking the bus."

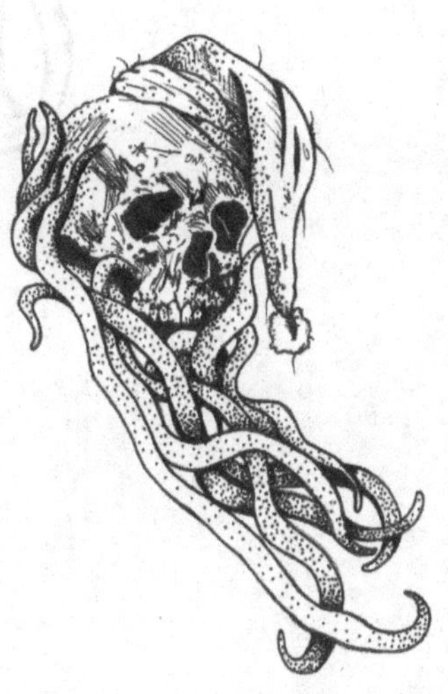

NAUGHTY NORMAN

There was no mistake.

Norman rubbed his eyes, thinking the gloom might have been playing tricks on him. Or was it the half bottle of whisky in his gut?

No.

He was real, hunched over, jostling through a large sack.

The yellow rays of light that seeped in through the living room window gave hints to a frizzled, white beard.

"I know you're there, Norman. You can stop hiding in the shadows," Santa said.

Norman hesitated then stepped out of the hallway. "I-I-I can't believe it," he said with a dry throat. Sweat covered every inch of him, the loose drapes of his checkered pyjamas stuck to his legs and arms, making them itch. "You're really real!"

"Why would there be any doubt?" Santa said, straightening and turning to him.

He was huge. Not just big, but almost giant-like. *Seven foot at least,* Norman thought as his heart quickened.

"I-I wanted things. Y-You never came," Norman said.

"That was a surprise to you?" Santa said, resting his huge hands on his hips.

"Well, I—"

"Come now, Norman. As a child, you were as naughty as they came. Stealing baseball cards. Bullying poor Kenny Jarrett; he's still seeking therapy for your constant thefts during grade school. He might be a successful real estate agent now, but he still frowns at his scarred feet. Remember the firecracker you hid in his sneakers?"

"It was just a joke," Norman said with a shrug, but knew it was vengeance. "He told on—"

"—and so he should have!" Santa said, his voice a little louder. "Too bad that Kenny wasn't the *only* one to suffer your brutal, stealing behaviours."

Norman lowered his head, remembering the other incident.

When he was twelve, he tried to trade baseball cards with Ricky Burke; he had a popular Roger Clemens card but wasn't trading it for anything. So he'd dragged Ricky out to the street, stretched out his left arm over the concrete gutter, and brought his foot down on it like he was breaking a heavy stick. He stole the card and swapped it weeks later for one of Craig Biggio.

"Norman. . ." Santa sighed, nodding his head, as though hearing his thoughts. "So naughty for silly cards."

"I know. But if I was so bad, why are you here?"

Santa huffed out a small laugh. "Well, although you were a menace, you have somehow managed to raise a delightfully good, little girl."

"Sarah?"

"Indeed. She shares her toys, helps children in class, and has been known to help the odd old lady across the street. Sometimes, things like this can't be explained. Your daughter is an angel, so I'm here for her."

"What have you brought?"

Norman watched as the giant man in red leant down to his sack and lifted a long gift, ornately wrapped in paper flecked with gold and red stars, and tied with a thin, curly ribbon.

The gift unwrapped on its own, as though by invisible hands, revealing a boxed Barbie Doll by Stefano Canturi. The white jewels around the small neck sparkled when they caught the light.

"Th-That doll. . . that can't be found any—"

"—are you forgetting who I am?"

Norman lowered his head.

"Your daughter deserves the best," Santa said as the paper and ribbon wrapped and wound itself around the expensive collector's doll.

Santa placed it beneath Norman's tattered excuse for a Christmas tree.

Norman cowered a little as Santa rose, staring down at him. "Try and be good, Norman. You're doing something right to have such a kind little girl. Be good, now?"

"Yes."

Norman watched as Santa and his sack transformed into an array of gold sparkles. Like a swarm of bees, the sparkles swirled around him and raced up the chimney.

Norman waited for endless moments, collected the gift from under the tree and raced upstairs to the tired computer by his bed.

The doll would fetch a great price on eBay.

The Well And The Snow

"I have to go out," Papa would say. "I need to sell some goods so we can eat. You look after Muma, keep warm, and don't go outside. It's too cold."

Papa sold ropes, used clothes and tools for yard work, just to name a few things. He would never let me go with him. "Too cold and harsh for a little girl," he would say. Muma would always be by the fire, mending clothes for Papa to sell, or over the cooker, stirring the turnips she saved from the ice outside. Home didn't feel like home anymore. Ever since Garret, a boy down in the village, spoke of a death in our well.

"That's right," he said through fat lips. "A boy died there, he did. His name was Esau. His step-daddy couldn't feed him anymore, folks say. So, he lynched him over the well. Cut him loose when his legs stopped twitching!"

I was disgusted by Garret *and* his story, but I couldn't help being spooked as Muma and I walked down the muddy road back to the cabin.

I peered at the well through a cracked glass window. Out in the yard, drizzled with snow, sat the circular formation of stones. My heart froze when I spotted my little teddy on the ground being layered with snowfall.

I'd forgotten it out there when I went to help Muma pick some turnips. Papa bought it for me from the village. My foolishness made my cheeks burn; how could I forget my teddy? I stepped out into the twilight, my feet sank into the snow up to my ankles, but I kept going; I had to bring my teddy back inside.

With every step, the well drew nearer.

Images of a blind-folded boy, hanging from a rope, invaded my eyes. The wind carried a woeful howl, as though some distant voice was screaming. Before I reached the well, I tripped over a rock hidden by the snow, and fell flat on my face. When I tried to get up, my heart hammered. The snow around me was moving.

Fissures grew, and the snow began to lump and form as if being sculpted by invisible hands. First, a roundish heap took place, then a larger bulge beneath it. After that, snow from the surrounds had drawn to the forming shapes like a vacuum. The mounds, one on top of the other, had grown just larger than me.

Other things came.

A broken, heavily-pecked carrot from nearby dragged itself to the mounds. In tow were an array of pebbles and leaves, all following the carrot like a line of marching ants. They dragged themselves up the mounds and settled upon the top-most heap.

My eyes widened to see they'd formed an emotionless face.

It stared at me with its black-pebble eyes.

I snapped my gaze to a grouping of sticks that slid their way to the mounds. Creeping and twisting up, they poked into the sides to mimic a pair of twiggy arms.

I lurched back when the whole form fell forward. I thought it had collapsed, but it was bending over. It jostled its sticky arms in the snow and rose.

My teddy was clasped in its hands.

"For me?" I asked it.

Its head wobbled forward and back.

I took it and ran back to the cabin as fast as I could.

A moment later, I braved the snow again. Reaching the well, I found that the mounds with the face had moved closer to the tree line.

"Esau!" I called. The top mound turned, revealing its face.

I ran to it and wrapped Papa's old scarf around its neck. I then placed an old, tattered hat on its head. "Merry Christmas," I said.

One of its twiggy arms lifted its hat to me and he turned away.

Esau visits me every Christmas.

I give him a new hat and scarf.

He smiles now.

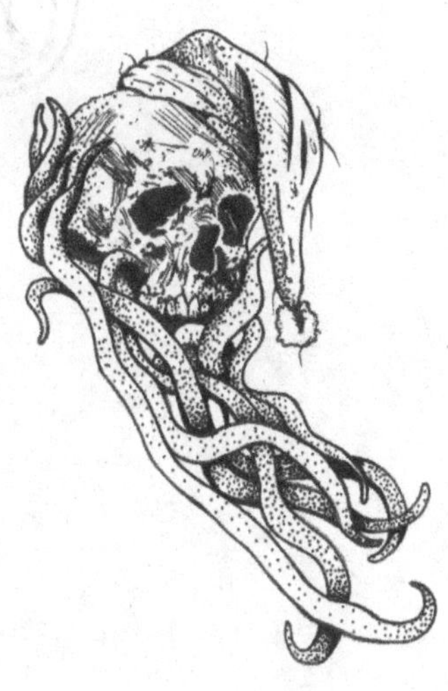

The Black Father Of The Night

Translated from the original Finnish

From trunk to branch, shrub to root,
Their bones we will grind to mix with flour,
Their claws we will bind, their throats be slit,
They will hang and drain for an hour.

Through the night they fly, through the dark they run,
They are the hardest to catch, but only for some,
We are quick, we are hungry, and we work and we bite,
Oh, how we feast—how we feast on this night. . .
—the song of Vrant and Kull.

Viborg, Finland, 1901.

Night crows called ominously from the roofs of smoke-cottages.

Darkness settled. The winds began to gust and the local merchant in the watchtower shivered with unease. The crows always sing their most foreboding songs in the time between Christmas Eve and Christmas Day. When young hearts are filled with joy, an unknown dread dwells in the small hearts of the wild—local hounds howl at the moon more so this eve. The merchant beats his drum. Townsfolk finished up their business and hurried indoors, seeking refuge from the snow and the night.

Not all obeyed the watchman's advice. Little Markus, his pink feet within wooden clogs, wandered about in the snow-covered cobbled streets. He stood beneath the glow of one of the street lanterns, gazing up at the star-filled sky: *When will the gift-giver be soaring?* His ears flexed suddenly to distant footsteps; his mother called through the cold, "Come inside at once!"

The watchman's drum echoed. Wrapped in a large shawl, Markus' mother approached. "Come, Markus!" She cuddled him into the warmth of her garments. Markus wanted to stay, to see the gift-giver fly, yet he was seduced by the comfort, ever devoted. She walked him back down the street toward their home.

"It is so cold! Why must you wander? Neither brave, nor smart . . . you will come to ill!" she complained as they reached the gate.

"I was watching, Mumma. Tonight he might come?"

They entered the yard; frozen rose bushes lined the fence. His mother paused; hiding her anger behind her closed, thin lips.

"Mumma? I am not naughty, nor bad? He will give to me this time?" he whimpered.

She knelt and looked into his big eyes; a smile did nothing to stop his sorrow.

"Maybe, my dear," she said as tenderly as she could. "He goes through much toil, this night… many houses… many children… over moon, through stars—"

"But, I've been good, Mumma!" Markus cried as he fell into her arms.

"I know you have, my dear," she whispered into his neck. "Listen to me. Come morning, if your stocking stays empty, fail you not the one thing you have."

"What be that?" he cried into his little hands.

"Me."

Leena embraced her son in the cold before taking him to warm by the fire.

Markus woke to merry strains of old Christmas rhymes echoing from the town's square. Snowflakes fluttered past his parchment window, creating dancing shadows on his bedroom wall—it had to be a worthy sign. He flung the blankets aside and leapt from his bed, hope alive in his heart as he took the stairs two at a time, his mind imagining the possibilities of what the gift-giver might have brought: toy wagon, wooden horse, candy… something *new*, something *his*. A toy that would allow him to play with the other children, share in their laughter, their friendship, not watch from the hedges again. It *had* to be his turn to receive from the gift-giver.

Markus' shoulders slumped. His stocking, hung with such belief above the fireplace the night before was empty.

Markus cried as he fell to his knees. Leena ran from her

stove. "My dear, you have risen so early." She cradled him. "There, there…" He bawled into her chest, his tears wetting her garment. "Look, Mumma has something for you."

Leena eased her trembling son back, fetching something from her dress pocket as she did so. He watched through his fingers, confused. Leena held in her hand a toffee she had bought from the market the day before. She placed it in his little palm. "Here. Say now, my son, for my ears to hear… You do not need *his* gifts."

"Naughty… I am!"

"No, no, you are not. You are a sweet boy!"

She embraced him again. "You *are* good, dear Markus!"

His mother stroked his hair—the toffee had begun to melt in his grasp. "Other boys and girls get his gifts!" he cried. "Why not give unto me! The others tease, Mumma."

"Whence the tears have dried, pain slips away in its stead," she said determinedly. "Settle into my arms, my love, it is your one painless place."

Beneath the wooden beams of Markus' bedroom, Leena sang her son to sleep with a lullaby; the same one her mother used to sing to her. Leena always held back her tears whenever she sang it, but her dear little boy loved it so. His deep, slow breaths made her sure he was fast asleep, and she blew out his candle, gathering her coat. Being as quiet as a mouse, she tiptoed down the old stairs. Venturing out with a determined pace, the dark of Christmas night swallowed her.

The drumming from the watchman's tower echoed through the streets and trailed her into the dense mountain forest like prowling movements. The late chill ate at her skin, the snow dragged at her feet, and the shadows ruled the secret path, but nothing would preclude her... The Nightjars and Rainbow bugs fell silent. A foul noise drifted on the wind, igniting her fear and quickening her heart. She scurried down the secret path, dread chilling her marrow.

A wave of heat swelled through Leena's shoulders as the little voices swirled around her, voices she hated, voices that still troubled her sleep. They'd mocked her when she was little, and they would persist until she shed tears. As she walked, she drew nearer to the creatures she had not seen for many years.

Their wicked songs lingered and strayed from the path into the twisting wood. She followed them, trying to control her fear. A rotten smell threatened her nose. Their foul little bodies were moving up ahead in a small clearing. Leena shifted a branch or two to feast her eyes on their camp. A fire was alive and cracking. Around it they danced.

Sickly songs spilled from their cracked lips, their black teeth like rotten candy against the orange glow of the fire. Their naked skin, darkened by years of chimney ash, their bony limbs, their dangling sex; their small leather belts, with a sheath strapped to each that housed their rusty little daggers. They were the father's helpers, wretched and grim, one was named Kull, and the other named Vrant, and together they would sing and they would chant:

> *We will pluck them, we will skin them,*
> *we will boil them in a stew,*
> *We will herb them,*
> *we will brew them and on their flesh we will chew!*

Mutilated night crows and hares lay dead around the fire. A large cloth sack wriggled and bulged. *A naughty child.* Leena's heart raced.

The little murderers, she thought as her mind wandered back. When she was not yet seven, she first spied on them. Once, they had beaten a poor child until he died in the weeds. Year after year, Leena tried to put a stop to their evils, but her courage always faltered. Instead, she would cry and watch from the shadows… Her young eyes witnessed them rip arms and legs from children and gut them whilst they still had the strength to scream, their bodies trembling as their brief lives drained onto the forest floor. Their breaths reduced to tiny gasps, as death would take them away, leaving in their place a feast for the dirty monsters.

Leena cleared her throat and stepped into the clearing, her face hot with outrage. They stopped their prancing by the flames, crouched over their dead, and began to pull the feathers and bite the fur. Melodies hummed from their lips and one even grunted and shat in the earth. Their little eyes darted with annoyance, but they kept about their work, and sang again as if no disturbance was brought.

> *We will cool them, we will cut them,*
> *we will serve them with bread,*
> *We will turn them,*
> *we will sauce them and bite off their heads!*

"A demon spat onto the waters, and out you both came."

Leena stepped further into view, her heart quickening into overdrive. She glanced at the moving cloth sack, and they hunched over it, guarding it like wolves over fresh prey. They hissed at her, drool stringing through their rotten black teeth.

"Not tonight!" she yelled.

"Ours! Our right! Our catch!" they spat in unison.

"Release the child, or joint from joint, I will undo you both!"

She stepped closer to their wretched bodies—she was not a little girl anymore. She towered over them, and knew in her determined heart that she could crush them.

Kull and Vrant laughed, mocked, and spat at her feet. They circled her, and sang a rhyme that used to send her crying to her mother.

> *Oh, Leena, Leena—Leena the small.*
> *You have the legs of a pig and the face of a troll.*
> *You are weak, you are ugly; you are nothing at all.*
> *Leena, Leena—how we love to watch you fall.*

"Free the child!"

"Ours!"

Vrant stormed in front of her and snarled and spat. He pulled out his dagger and thrashed it across her bulk. A sharp pain struck her thigh and she lost her balance and fell on her rear.

"You are not welcome, you filthy little whore! I will drain you. I will eat you! My teeth through your skin like a saw!"

Vrant's dagger raised, its point destined for her gut. A thrash from the darkness sent him cowering by Kull. A tall and large figure entered the clearing, wielding a pointed staff, and through its beard came a vexed gruff. Vrant and Kull trembled in the blackness of its shadow as the fire gave hints of its form. "Father?" they both trembled. "Always, we honour you!"

"Be silent!" the father yelled in his deep voice. "Take your feast into the dark! Be off with you!"

Leena got to her feet, nursing her stinging wound. It was long, but she chose not to let it burden her. "The child! The child!" she protested.

"Ours to take!" claimed Vrant and Kull.

"The sack will remain!" the father ordered.

They both looked up at him with the eyes of sad hounds. "But, Father?"

"Your birds and your hares shall rest within your wretched arms. The child will live to steal bread another day… perhaps another will lay in bad luck's bed next year, but not this night."

Vrant and Kull snarled and sobbed, gathering their raw feast, and scurrying into the dark woods, cursing as they went. Leena hurried to the sack, her fingers trembling as she untied it. A young girl was inside, not much older than Markus. Screaming and kicking out of her cloth prison, she ran back to the way of the town.

"Little monsters, how could you still let them prey on the young?"

He stood over her in silence, his face shrouded in shadow. "They have their uses."

"They are vermin!"

"They are loyal… and they only ask for one night to feast… this night."

"How dare you grant it!"

"Leave now… I have a fire to feed and some warmth to gain," he dismissed. Turning his back on her, the woods then swallowed him.

Leena rushed after him but said nothing; she wanted to talk face to face, not gasp and chase him for answers.

The moonlight shone over his hidden, wooden cottage, which rested by the roots of the mountain. Smoke billowed from its little chimney, and night crows called from nearby trees. Attached to the cottage was his workshop, and across the way, through a yard of overgrown shrubbery, was the stable.

The noisy slumber of Sleipnir caught her ears; the father's eight-legged horse, mistaken by the townsfolk as a group of reindeer. Sleipnir was menacing to feast eyes upon, but was easily tameable with a gentle stroke to the mane and a bucket full of carrots.

The father, although not acknowledging her chase, entered his cottage, leaving the door ajar. When Leena shut the wooden door behind her, the familiar scent of rum and dusted timber caught her cherry nose. The cottage looked as she had remembered. The boards were recently swept and the roof beams were clear of any cobwebs. She stepped down the dark hall, boards creaking beneath her feet, and into the dimly lit living room. The father was warming his large hands by the open fire, his staff resting on his armchair. "Nothing to my ears, have you to say?" she asked her father.

"I see you still service other men in their beds."

"What choice do I have? I need to bring shelter and warmth to my son."

"Away with you."

Leena stepped closer. "Why do you ignore him? He is your child!"

"Poison, his very body. He is the symbol of my flaws. I am mending my ways. Split asunder it will be if I choose to grant him."

"Punishing him for your own evils? Hate me if you must, but how dare you neglect him. He longs to have the treasures that are anointed to the other children at Christmas. A gift? A blessing? He is lonely, Father. He feels worthless!"

"If this is why you have come, then leave," he said, turning around. "If he is feeling such a way, then as a mother, you have failed."

"How dare you!" Leena stomped over to him and smacked him across his wide face.

He did not retaliate. He stood frozen, clutching his throbbing cheek with his large hand. He stared at her with wild dark eyes. His stare granted a stab of pity for him, but the longer she looked, the more she despised.

"Unto the pit of a pig, lays a neater place." She looked him up and down, hands on her hips. "The townsfolk claim you as a God; *'The gift-giver'; a saint?* Songs to end all songs, they would sing. Little do they see the swine, the old man, the one who used to call himself my father. The one who filled me with his seed."

"Stop this."

"You scared hog, in a beard and dress. Hiding behind myth, surrounding yourself with the filth you call your helpers. Teased and tortured I was, for years when I lived here, and you did nothing! Mother was the only one who cared."

"You will not speak of your mother!" the large man yelled.

"Why not? Ignorant was she? About your evils? The evils in my bed?"

"No! She had no knowledge!"

"You are so sure of this? This place is small, Father." She teased in the cruellest voice; the anger was fuming in her, giving her strength. "There is no silence here, nowhere evils can hide. Mother heard you, breathing and panting. To you it was honey, but to her it was venom. She heard my pleas, but feared to do anything. That is why she dove into the river of death—"

"You little whore!" He backhanded her, knocking her to the floor.

Cheek throbbing, blood soured her tongue. He kicked into her ribs and flipped her onto her back. She tried to rise but he slammed his boot down on her left hand. It hurt, her wrist straining beneath his weight. Her right hand was pinned with his other boot as he leered down at her, triumphant.

"Let me up, Father!"

"Your mother was taken by the blizzard and that is the end of it!"

"If that comforts you, then believe what you wish. But it is knowledge to us both that she ran out into that storm, willing it to swallow her!"

"You little witch!" He stamped his foot into her belly.

Leena gasped.

"Leave!" The father stepped back to his place before the fire. Trembling with anger, he held his large hands again before it. "Leave and never return."

Leena struggled to her feet, gathering the blood thick in her mouth. She spat on his armchair with malevolence. He marched over to her with thundering steps and gripped her shoulders, forcing her against him. "How dare you!"

"In hell, may your flesh and veins be torn!" She turned her face from the stench of rum and spittle that fouled his beard.

The father groaned; he had never forgotten the smell of her hair, her breath, her sweat—it always aroused him. "I can grant a cure for loneliness to the boy—" he pressed his face to hers "—I, a man of great gifts."

"No…" she whispered, his stink and words suffocating her fragile spirit. "Please, stop."

His tongue snaked out of his mouth and stroked her earlobe. The sound of his bubbling saliva and the heat of his tongue forced her to dry retch.

She struggled to free herself but was held in place.

"You should never have come here."

He threw her to the floor.

Leena tried to get to her feet, but the weight of her father was upon her.

What would become of the emptiness in his little heart? Markus sweated in his bed, stirring and muttering in troubled slumber. He called for his mother. She answered him from down the stairs. He rushed to her, finding her resting before the dead fireplace. It was cold in the house; he could see his breaths. A layer of smoke billowed from the starving coals.

He went down to her and she was weak with red cheeks. He huddled within her arms and found warmth again; a warmth that would never fail him. A fast heartbeat drummed into his ear from the inside of her chest and an unwelcoming smell stung his nostrils. "Have you come to ill, Mumma?"

"Maybe for a time," she breathed. "Rise up from despair, my son. I will be well again soon."

"Where have you been, Mumma?"

She let out a trembling breath and uttered, "To see the gift-giver…"

"You did?" He rose from her embrace. "Found for me a toy, Mumma?"

"No. There are no toys there in his evil place." She cupped his face. "Promise me now, my son, you will *not* long for his gifts again. You must hate him, now. He is wicked. He is evil, and so too are his servants."

Markus' eyes welled. "That cannot be true, Mumma?"

"It is, my love. It is time for hate now, not tears."

"Why?"

"Because we know the truth that they are wicked, and when the time is right, we will seek them out."

Markus stared at his mother; disbelief trembled his bottom lip.

Leena took Markus' cold hand and placed it over her belly, whispering, "Feel it, it is a-growing. We must wait until your sibling grows, my dear… Together, the three of us will enter the cursed lands of their forest. We must wait and be angry for many years, until you have the hands and strength of a man, and be not of a child.

"The wicked ones will be frailer with their souls decaying, and they *will* lose the war that we will beset upon them."

Markus cried into his Mumma's arms; her hard and cold words were unfamiliar to his little ears.

"There, there, my darling," Leena returned some tender tones to her voice. "Your poor little mind does not understand, but it will in time and so will the mind of the newborn. In the dark of one future Christmas Eve, the gift-giver and his wretched servants will be cast into the river of death."

She stroked his hair as he cried further into her bosom. "Then your sibling will craft with you, care for you as you take the name of 'Nickolas,' and be forever more, the man of great gifts."

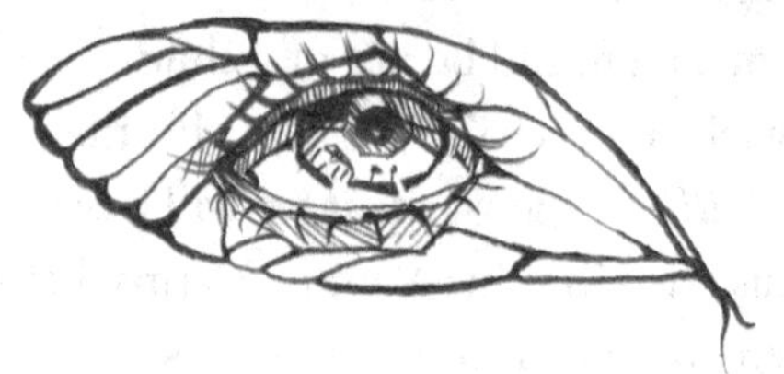

Acknowledgements

The book you hold in your hands would not have been possible if it weren't for the original believers in its right to exist. I give a heartfelt thanks to Ashley and Brooke from Close Up Books, for being the first publishers of the first edition, *Beneath the Ferny Tree*. The book had seen great coverage and had even earned a nomination for best collected work in the Australasian Shadows Awards in 2018. That was a thrill to be present and see the book being read out to the audience amongst the other nominees.

A huge thank you goes to my editor, Amanda J Spedding from Phoenix Editing. Your support and friendship over the many years has been invaluable, and your magic has weaved colour to my web of creepy, grey words.

Having the support of the community in the Australasian Horror Writers Association has helped me shine, and if you would like anyone to blame for my wild ideas and numerous on-page monstrosities, please see Marty Young, the mad scientist and horror author who mentored me in my beginnings. Your belief in my madness was there at the start, and when I fell down after one too many rejections, you were there to drag me up and say, "No one quits in this man's army!" You made me stronger as an author, my friend, so thank you!

There have been numerous publishers since *Beneath*

the Ferny Tree was released, so there are too many 'thank you' notes to place here, but I have noted your support for my work in the copyright page, so to all of the editors and publishers within those houses, I send my warmest regards for the opportunity to be showcased within your respective publications.

This new expanded edition, now obviously retitled, begins with a beautiful introduction from Geoff Brown and Dawn Roach from Cohesion Press. You both have never failed to welcome me with open arms whenever I had questions regarding the publishing of this new book, your support to *all* of my creativity and, at times, wacky silliness with the patience that feels like family. May Asylumfest continue to grow and our association and friendship with it. Thank you for encouraging me to pursue *Careful With That Axe*, and for gracing the first pages with your kind words.

To the team at Asylum Ghost Tours, past and present, you know who you all are and I always look forward to seeing you each year.

To all of my friends who share my family dinner table, board games, movie viewings, writing retreats, role plays, camping, gym sessions, coffee dates, walks, dog walks, walks with coffee, walks with dogs and coffee... you all mean so much to me and I value your friendship.

My family in Australia and around the world, you are always there supporting my artwork and literary achievements and progress work. It is wonderful to live in an age where one can share their creativity and have it land before your eyes in real-time. Your support is warmly received and always gives me a smile.

To my own family. My soul supporter and love of my life, Rhonda, your support and honesty regarding my work is always inspiring and brings out the best in me and I couldn't achieve it without you. And my two awesome humans, Anthony and Eve, without your love and support, none of this would mean much at all.

Lastly, to my readers. It goes without saying how important you all are and now that I am attending events, it is truly a pleasure to be in your presence. You keep coming back and so that means after the many years of creepy stories and art, you've forgiven me. I love you all.

Until next time,

Dave

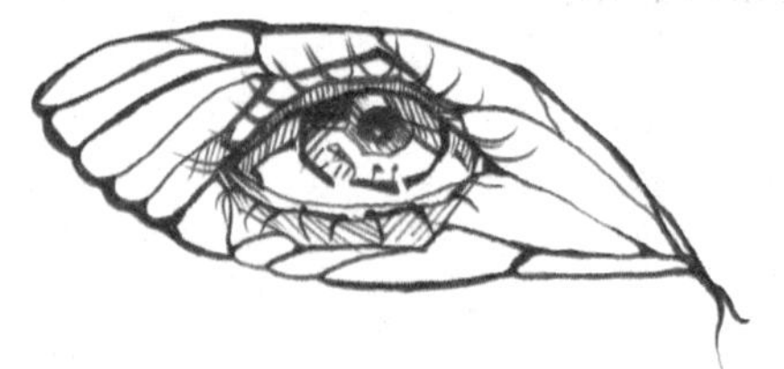

BIOGRAPHY

David Schembri is an *award-nominated author, artist, comic creator and poet from Australia. He is the author of *Unearthly Fables* (The Writing Show, 2013), *Beneath The Ferny Tree* (Close-Up Books, 2018), and the comics, *Splitting Sides: Tales of Humorous Horror #1, *#2 and #3, Crowman #1* and *Val the Vampire #1*.

His first novella will be released soon by Odyssey Books.

David's short fiction has been published by Chaosium Inc, Horror World Press, Things in the Well, Black Beacon Books and Midnight Echo.

His poetry has appeared in several issues of the Hippocampus Press review, *Spectral Realms*, edited by S.T. Joshi. His poem, *Shadow and Fire* (published in the Winter issue of *Spectral Realms*) had made Ellen Datlaow's longlist for best horror of 2022. Other poetry appearances are also noted within the *Anno KlarkAsh-Ton Anthology* by Rainfall Books, issue 13 of *Midnight Echo* and Issue 55 of *Silver Blade Magazine.*

davidschembri.net

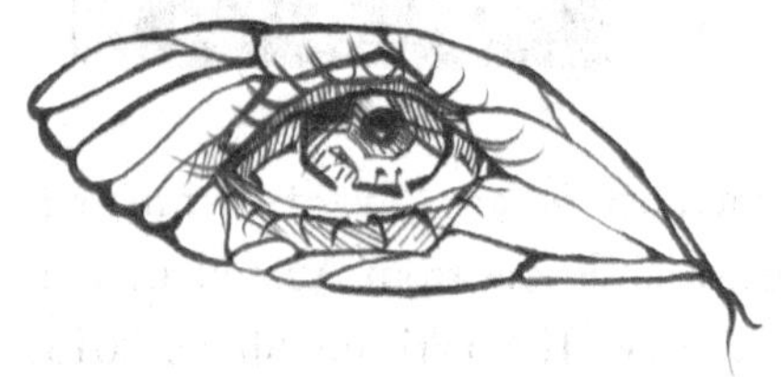

ALSO BY DAVID SCHEMBRI

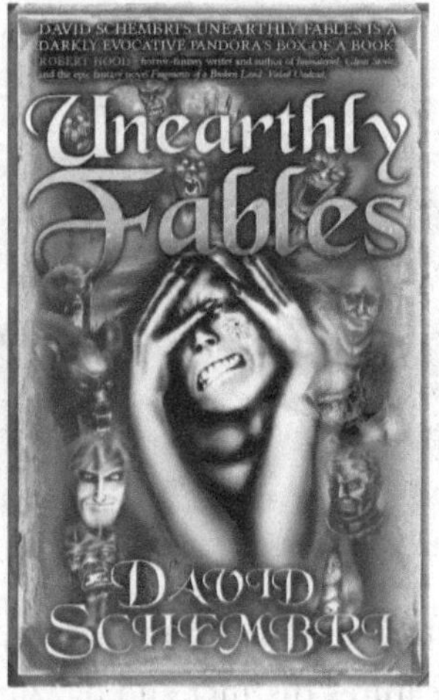

Within these parchments lie places hidden from the world. Where demons dance, hope is forsaken and dear is relished. Enter at your own risk …

This collection of horror stories and artwork can be purchased from most online book stores in both paper back and digital editions.

Available on **amazon** and most online retailers!

Comics by David Schembri

Splitting Sides: Tales of Humorous Horror

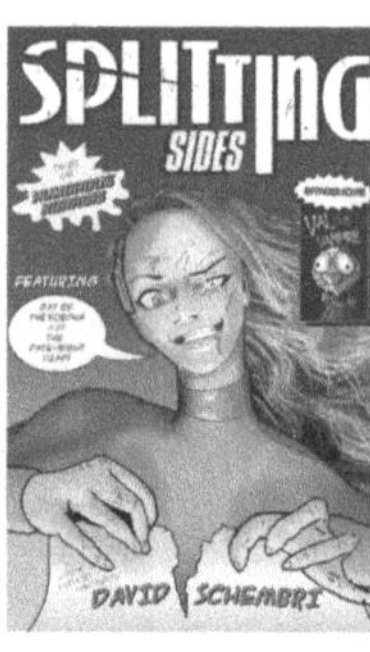

Based on the stories from horror writer, David Schembri, *Splitting Sides* features distinct and dazzling illustrations by the author along with his darkly humorous tribute to horror comics of the 50s.

Along with some delightfully entertaining advertisements, these comics will leave you horrified and giggling at the same time. Sit back and enjoy these instalments, providing you with a glimpse into the crazy reaches of David's mind.

Available on **amazon** and most online retailers!

Crowman: The Return of Mr Mosquito

Welcome to the first issue of *Crowman*, and better still, it's a colouring book! Follow him as he encounters a strange villain from his past. Will this be his final showdown? Will he live to fight another day? Will the city be in desperate need for another protector if things go sour? Turn the pages, colour them in, and find out.

Available on **amazon** and most online retailers!

Val The Vampire

As seen in *Splitting Sides* Issue #1, *Val the Vampire* is offered here as a separate comic. His first two episodes, along with some daily comic strips, will be sure to tickle your funny bones.

Available directly from the author only.

Signed hard copies of David's entire library can be arranged and shipped to you directly. Just tap him a message on Facebook or contact him via the website below. Happy reading! *davidschembri.net*

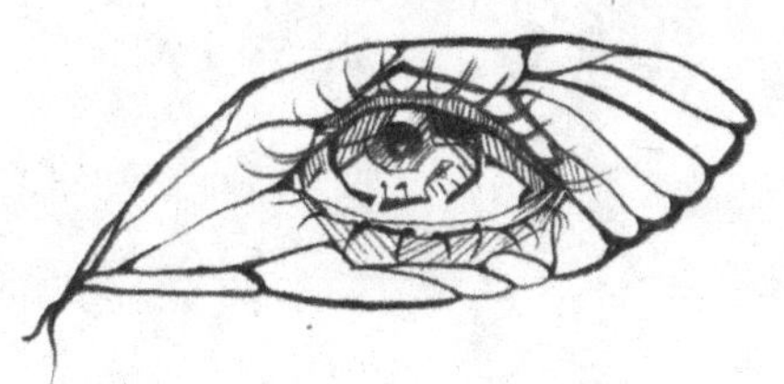